Marx Hardy Joyce
Defoe Abbott Melville Machiavelli Montaigne Chesterton Cooper Emerson Austen
Stoker Carroll Christie Haggard Haggard Hugo
Wilde Maupassant Byron Eliot Grimm
Garnett Engels Schiller Molière
Goethe Einstein Fitzgerald Hawthorne Smith Kafka
Baum Cotton Kipling Doyle Hall
Henry Dostoyevsky Willis
Leslie Dumas Flaubert Turgenev Nietzsche Balzac
Stockton Vatsyayana Crane
Burroughs Verne
Curtis Tocqueville Whitman Gogol Vinci
Homer Widger Tolstoy Busch
Darwin Thoreau Twain Scott Harte
Potter Freud Zola Lawrence Plato
Kant Jowett Stevenson Dickens Hesse
Andersen Cervantes Burton
London Descartes Voltaire
Poe Aristotle Wells Cooke
Hale James Hastings
Bunner Shakespeare Irving
Richter Chambers da Shaw
Doré Dante Chekhov Wodehouse Benedict Alcott
Swift Pushkin
Newton

 tredition®

tredition was established in 2006 by Sandra Latusseck and Soenke Schulz. Based in Hamburg, Germany, tredition offers publishing solutions to authors and publishing houses, combined with world-wide distribution of printed and digital book content. tredition is uniquely positioned to enable authors and publishing houses to create books on their own terms and without conventional manu-facturing risks.

For more information please visit: www.tredition.com

TREDITION CLASSICS

This book is part of the TREDITION CLASSICS series. The creators of this series are united by passion for literature and driven by the intention of making all public domain books available in printed format again - worldwide. Most TREDITION CLASSICS titles have been out of print and off the bookstore shelves for decades. At tredition we believe that a great book never goes out of style and that its value is eternal. Several mostly non-profit literature projects provide content to tredition. To support their good work, tredition donates a portion of the proceeds from each sold copy. As a reader of a TREDITION CLASSICS book, you support our mission to save many of the amazing works of world literature from oblivion. See all available books at www.tredition.com.

Project Gutenberg

The content for this book has been graciously provided by Project Gutenberg. Project Gutenberg is a non-profit organization founded by Michael Hart in 1971 at the University of Illinois. The mission of Project Gutenberg is simple: To encourage the creation and distribu-tion of eBooks. Project Gutenberg is the first and largest collection of public domain eBooks.

The Intellectual Development of the Canadian People

John George, Sir Bourinot

Imprint

This book is part of TREDITION CLASSICS

Author: John George, Sir Bourinot
Cover design: Buchgut, Berlin – Germany

Publisher: tredition GmbH, Hamburg - Germany
ISBN: 978-3-8424-6321-9

www.tredition.com
www.tredition.de

Copyright:
The content of this book is sourced from the public domain.

The intention of the TREDITION CLASSICS series is to make world literature in the public domain available in printed format. Literary enthusiasts and organizations, such as Project Gutenberg, world-wide have scanned and digitally edited the original texts. tredition has subsequently formatted and redesigned the content into a modern reading layout. Therefore, we cannot guarantee the exact reproduction of the original format of a particular historic edition. Please also note that no modifications have been made to the spelling, therefore it may differ from the orthography used today.

PREFATORY NOTE.

This series of papers has been prepared in accordance with a plan marked out by the writer, some years ago of taking up, from time to time, certain features of the social, political and industrial progress of the Dominion. Essays on the Maritime Industry and the National Development of Canada have been read before the Royal Colonial Institute in England, and have been so favourably received by the Press of both countries, that the writer has felt encouraged to continue in the same course of study, and supplement his previous efforts by an historical review of the intellectual progress of the Canadian people.

HOUSE OF COMMONS, OTTAWA, February 17th, 1881.

CONTENTS.

CHAPTER I.

EFFECT OF SOCIAL AND POLITICAL CHANGES ON MENTAL DEVELOPMENT.

CHAPTER II.

EDUCATION.

CHAPTER III.

JOURNALISM.

CHAPTER IV.

NATIVE LITERATURE.

CHAPTER I.

EFFECT OF SOCIAL AND POLITICAL CHANGES ON MENTAL DEVELOPMENT.

Should the title of this review come by any chance under the notice of some of those learned gentlemen who are delving among Greek roots or working out abstruse mathematical problems in the great academic seats on the banks of the Cam or Isis, they would probably wonder what can be said on the subject of the intellectual development of a people engaged in the absorbing practical work of a Colonial dependency. To such eminent scholars Canada is probably only remarkable as a country where even yet there is, apparently, so little sound scholarship that vacancies in classical and mathematical chairs have to be frequently filled by gentlemen who have distinguished themselves in the Universities of the parent state. Indeed, if we are to judge from articles and books that appear from time to time in England with reference to this country, Englishmen in general know very little of the progress that has been made in culture since Canada has become the most important dependency of Great Britain, by virtue of her material progress within half a century. Even the Americans who live alongside of us, and would be naturally supposed to be pretty well informed as to the progress of the Dominion to their north, appear for the most part ignorant of the facts of its development in this particular. It was but the other day that a writer of some ability, in an organ of religious opinion, referred to the French Canadians as a people speaking only inferior French, and entirely wanting in intellectual vigour. Nor is this fact surprising when we consider that there are even some Canadians who do not appear to have that knowledge which they ought to have on such a subject, and take many opportunities of concealing their ignorance by depreciating the intellectual efforts of their countrymen. If so much ignorance or indifference prevails with respect to the progress of Canada in this respect, it must be admitted—

however little flattering the admission may be to our national pride — that it is, after all, only the natural sequel of colonial obscurity. It is still a current belief abroad — at least in Europe — that we are all so much occupied with the care of our material interests, that we are so deeply absorbed by the grosser conditions of existence in a new country, that we have little opportunity or leisure to cultivate those things which give refinement and tone to social life. Many persons lose sight of the fact that Canada, young though she is compared with the countries of the Old World, has passed beyond the state of mere colonial pupilage. One very important section of her population has a history contemporaneous with the history of the New England States, whose literature is read wherever the English tongue is spoken. The British population have a history which goes back over a century, and it is the record of an industrious, enterprising people who have made great political and social progress. Indeed it may be said that the political and material progress that these two sections of the Canadian people have conjointly made is of itself an evidence of their mental capacity. But whilst reams are written on the industrial progress of the Dominion with the praiseworthy object of bringing additional capital and people into the country, only an incidental allusion is made now and then to the illustrations of mental activity which are found in its schools, in its press, and even in its literature. It is now the purpose of the present writer to show that, in the essential elements of intellectual development, Canada is making not a rapid but certainly at least a steady and encouraging progress, which proves that her people have not lost, in consequence of the decided disadvantages of their colonial situation, any of the characteristics of the races to whom they owe their origin. He will endeavour to treat the subject in the spirit of an impartial critic, and confine himself as closely as possible to such facts as illustrate the character of the progress, and give much encouragement for the future of a country even now only a little beyond the infancy of its material as well as intellectual development.

It is necessary to consider first the conditions under which the Dominion has been peopled, before proceeding to follow the progress of intellectual culture. So far, the history of Canada may be divided into three memorable periods of political and social development. The first period lasted during the years of French dominion; the second, from the Conquest to the Union of 1840, during which the provinces were working out representative institutions; the third, from 1840 to 1867, during which interval the country enjoyed responsible government, and entered on a career of material progress only exceeded by that of the great nation on its borders. Since 1867, Canada has commenced a new period in her political development, the full results of which are yet a problem, but which the writer believes, in common with all hopeful Canadians, will tend eventually to enlarge her political condition, and place her in a higher position among communities. It is only necessary, however, to refer particularly to the three first periods in this introductory chapter, which is merely intended to show as concisely as possible those successive changes in the social and political circumstances of the provinces, which have necessarily had the effect of stimulating the intellectual development of the people.

Religion and commerce, poverty and misfortune, loyalty and devotion to the British Empire, have brought into the Dominion of Canada the people who, within a comparatively short period of time, have won from the wilderness a country whose present condition is the best evidence of their industrial activity. Religion was a very potent influence in the settlement of New France. It gave to the country — to the Indian as well as to the Frenchman — the services of a zealous, devoted band of missionaries who, with unfaltering courage, forced their way into the then trackless West, and associated their names to all time with the rivers, lakes, and forests of that vast region, which is now the most productive granary of the world. In the wake of these priestly pioneers followed the trader and adventurer to assist in solving the secrets of unknown rivers and illimitable forests. From the hardy peasantry of Normandy and Brittany came reinforcements to settle the lands on the banks of the St Lawrence and its tributary rivers, and lay the foundations of the present Province of Quebec. The life of the population, that, in the course of time, filled up certain districts of the province, was one of constant restlessness and uncertainty which prevented them ever attaining a permanent prosperity. When the French regime disappeared with the fall of Quebec and Montreal, it can hardly be said there existed a Canadian people distinguished for material or intellectual activity.

At no time under the government of France had the voice of the 'habitants' any influence in the councils of their country. A bureaucracy, acting directly under the orders of the King of France, managed public affairs; and the French Canadian of those times, very unlike his rival in New England, was a mere automaton, without any political significance whatever. The communities of people that were settled on the St. Lawrence and in Acadia were sunk in an intellectual lethargy—the natural consequence not only of their hard struggle for existence, but equally of their inability to take a part in the government of the country. It was impossible that a people who had no inducement to study public affairs—who could not even hold a town or parish meeting for the establishment of a public schools—should give many signs of mental vigour. Consequently, at the time of the Conquest, the people of the Canadian settlements seemed to have no aspirations for the future, no interest in the prosperity or welfare of each other, no real bonds of unity. The very flag which floated above them was an ever-present evidence of their national humiliation.

So the first period of Canadian history went down amid the deepest gloom, and many years passed away before the country saw the gleam of a brighter day. On one side of the English Channel, the King of France soon forgot his mortification at the loss of an unprofitable 'region of frost and snow;' on the other side, the English Government looked with indifference, now that the victory was won, on the acquisition of an alien people who were likely to be a source of trouble and expense. Then occurred the War of American Independence, which aroused the English Ministry from their indifference and forced into the country many thousands of resolute, intelligent men, who gave up everything in their devotion to one absorbing principle of loyalty. The history of these men is still to be written as respects their real influence on the political and social life of the Canadian Provinces. A very superficial review, however, of the characteristics of these pioneers will show that they were men of strong opinions and great force of character—valuable qualities in the formation of a new community. If, in their Toryism, they and their descendants were slow to change their opinions and to yield to the force of those progressive ideas necessary to the political and mental development of a new country, yet, perhaps, these were not dangerous characteristics at a time when republicanism had not a few adherents among those who saw the greater progress and prosperity of the people to the south of the St. Lawrence and the Great Lakes. These men were not ordinary immigrants, drawn from the ignorant, poverty-stricken classes of an Old World; they were men of a time which had produced Otis, Franklin, Adams, Hancock and Washington—men of remarkable energy and intellectual power. Not a few of these men formed in the Canadian colony little centres from which radiated more or less of intellectual light to brighten the prevailing darkness of those rough times of Canadian settlement. The exertions of these men, combined with the industry of others brought into the country by the hope of making homes and fortunes in the New World, opened up, in the course of years, the fertile lands of the West. Then two provinces were formed in the East and West, divided by the Ottawa River, and representative government was conceded to each. The struggles of the majority to enlarge their political liberties and break the trammels of a selfish bureaucracy illustrate the new mental vigour that was infused into the French Canadian race by the concession of the parliamentary system of 1792. The descendants of the people who had no share whatever in the government under French rule had at last an admirable opportunity of proving their capacity for administering their own affairs, and the verdict of the present is, that, on the whole, whatever mistakes were committed by their too ardent and impulsive leaders, they showed their full appreciation of the rights that were justly theirs as the people of a free colonial community. Their minds expanded with their new political existence, and a new people were born on the banks of the St. Lawrence.

At the same time the English-speaking communities of Upper Canada and the Maritime Provinces advanced in mental vigour with the progress of the struggle for more liberal institutions. Men of no ordinary intellectual power were created by that political agitation which forced the most indifferent from that, mental apathy, natural perhaps to a new country, where a struggle for mere existence demands such unflagging physical exertion. It is, however, in the new era that followed the Union that we find the fullest evidence of the decided mental progress of the Canadian communities. From that date the Canadian Provinces entered on a new period of industrial and mental activity. Old jealousies and rivalries between the different races of the country became more or less softened by the closer intercourse, social and political, that the Union brought about. During the fierce political conflicts that lasted for so many years in Lower Canada—those years of trial for all true Canadians—the division between the two races was not a mere line, but apparently a deep gulf, almost impossible to be bridged in the then temper of the contending parties. No common education served to remove and soften the differences of origin and language. The associations of youth, the sports of childhood, the studies by which the character of manhood is modified, were totally distinct. [Footnote: Report of Lord Durham on Canada, pp. 14-15.] With the Union of 1840, unpalatable as it was to many French Canadians who believed that the measure was intended to destroy their political autonomy, came a spirit of conciliation which tended to modify, in the course of no long time, the animosities of the past, and awaken a belief in the good will and patriotism of the two races, then working side by side in a common country, and having the same destiny in the future. And with the improvement of facilities for trade and intercourse, all sections were brought into those more intimate relations which naturally give an impulse not only to internal commerce but to the intellectual faculties of a people. [Footnote: Lord Macaulay says on this point: Every improvement of the means of locomotion benefits mankind morally and intellectually, as well as materially, and not only facilitates the interchange of the various productions of nature and art, but tends to remove natural and provincial antipathies and to bind together all the branches of the human family.] During the first years of the settlement of Canada there was a vast amount of ignorance throughout the rural districts, especially in the western Province. Travellers who visited the country and had abundant opportunities of ascertaining its social condition, dwelt pointedly on the moral and intellectual apathy that prevailed outside a few places like York or other centres of intelligence; but they forgot to make allowance for the difficulties that surrounded these settlers. The isolation of their lives had naturally the effect of making even the better class narrow-minded, selfish, and at last careless of anything like refinement. Men who lived for years without the means of frequent communication with their fellow-men, without opportunities for social, instructive intercourse, except what they might enjoy at rare intervals through the visit of some intelligent clergyman or tourist, might well have little ambition except to satisfy the grosser wants of their nature. The post office, the school, and the church were only to be found, in the majority of cases, at a great distance from their homes. Their children, as likely as not, grew up in ignorance, even were educational facilities at hand; for in those days the parent had absolute need of his son's assistance in the avocations of pioneer life. Yet, with all these disadvantages, these men displayed a spirit of manly independence and fortitude which was in some measure a test of their capacity for better things. They helped to make the country what it is, and to prepare the way for the larger population which came into it under more favourable auspices after the Union of 1840. From that time Canada received a decided impulse in everything that tends to make a country happy and prosperous. Cities, towns and villages sprang up with remarkable activity all over the face of the country, and vastly enlarged the opportunities for that social intercourse which is always an important factor in the education of a new country. At the same time, with the progress of the country in population and wealth, there grew up a spirit of self-reliance which of itself attested the mental vigour of the people. Whilst England was still for many 'the old home,' rich in memories of the past, Canada began to be a real entity, as it were, a something to be loved, and to be proud of. The only reminiscences that very many had of the countries of their origin were reminiscences of poverty and wretchedness, and this class valued above all old national associations the comfort and independence, if not wealth, they had been able to win in their Canadian home. The Frenchman, Scotchman, Irishman, and Englishman, now that they had achieved a marked success in their pioneer work, determined that their children should not be behind those of New England, and set to work to build up a system of education far more comprehensive and liberal than that enjoyed by the masses in Great Britain. On all sides at last there were many evidences of the progress of culture, stimulated by the more generally diffused prosperity. It was only necessary to enter into the homes of the people, not in the cities and important centres of industry and education, but in the rural districts, to see the effects of the industrial and mental development within the period that elapsed from the Union of 1840 to the Confederation of 1867. Where a humble log cabin once rose among the black pine stumps, a comfortable and in many cases expensive mansion, of wood or more durable material, had become the home of the Canadian farmer, who, probably, in his early life, had been but a poor peasant in the mother country. He himself, whose life had been one of unremitting toil and endeavour, showed no culture, but his children reaped the full benefits of the splendid opportunities of acquiring knowledge afforded by the country which owed its prosperity to their father and men like him. The homes of such men, in the most favoured districts, were no longer the abodes of rude industry, but illustrative, in not a few cases, of that comfort and refinement which must be the natural sequence of the general distribution of wealth, the improvement of internal intercourse, and the growth of education.

When France no longer owned a foot of land in British North America, except two or three barren islets on the coast of Newfoundland, the total population of the provinces known now as Canada was not above seventy thousand souls, nearly all French. From that time to 1840, the population of the different provinces made but a slow increase, owing to the ignorance that prevailed as to Canada, the indifference of English statesmen in respect to colonization, internal dissensions in the country itself, and its slow progress, as compared with the great republic on its borders. Yet, despite these obstacles to advancement, by 1841 the population of Canada reached nearly a million and a half, of whom at least fifty-five per cent. were French Canadians. Then the tide of immigration set in this direction, until at last the total population of Canada rose, in 1867, to between three and four millions, or an increase of more than a hundred per cent. in a quarter of a century. By the last Census of 1870, we have some idea of the national character of this population—more than eighty per cent. being Canadian by birth, and, consequently, identified in all senses of the term with the soil and prosperity of the country. Whilst the large proportion of the people are necessarily engaged in those industrial pursuits which are the basis of a country's material prosperity, the statistics show the rapid growth of the classes who live by mental labour, and who are naturally the leaders in matters of culture. The total number of the professional class in all the provinces was some 40,000, of whom 4,436 were clergymen, 109 judges, 264 professors, 3,000 advocates and notaries, 2,792 physicians and surgeons, 13,400 teachers, 451 civil engineers, 232 architects; and for the first time we find mention of a special class of artists and *litterateurs*, 590 in all, and these evidently do not include journalists, who would, if enumerated, largely swell the number.

Previous to 1867, different communities of people existed throughout British North America, but they had no general interest or purpose, no real bond of union, except their common allegiance to one Sovereign. The Confederation of the Provinces was intended, by its very essence and operation, to stimulate, not only the industrial energy, but the mental activity as well, of the different communities that compose the Dominion. A wider field of thought has, undoubtedly, been opened up to these communities, so long dwarfed by that narrow provincialism which every now and then crops up to mar our national development and impede intellectual progress. Already the people of the Confederated Provinces are every where abroad recognised as Canadians—as a Canadian people, with a history of their own, with certain achievements to prove their industrial activity. Climatic influences, all history proves, have much to do with the progress of a people. It is an admitted fact that the highest grade of intellect has always been developed, sooner or later, in those countries which have no great diversities of climate. [Footnote: Sir A. Alison (Vol. xiii. p. 271). says on this point: 'Canada and the other British possessions in British North America, though apparently blessed with fewer physical advantages than the country to the South, contain a noble race, and are evidently destined for a lofty destination. Everything there is in proper keeping for the development of the combined physical and mental qualities of man. There are to be found at once the hardihood of character which conquers difficulty, the severity of climate which stimulates exertion, and natural advantages which reward enterprise.'] If our natural conditions are favourable to our mental growth, so, too, it may be urged that the difference of races which exists in Canada may have a useful influence upon the moral as well as the intellectual nature of the people as a whole. In all the measures calculated to develop the industrial resources and stimulate the intellectual life of the Dominion, the names of French Canadians appear along with those of British origin. The French Canadian is animated by a deep veneration for the past history of his native country, and by a very decided determination to preserve his language and institutions intact; and consequently there exists in the Province of Quebec a national French Canadian sentiment, which has produced no mean intellectual fruits. We know that all the grand efforts in the attainment of civilization have been accomplished by a combination of different peoples. The union of the races in Canada must have its effect in the way of varying and reproducing, and probably invigorating also, many of the qualities belonging to each — material, moral, and mental; an effect only perceptible after the lapse of very many years, but which is, nevertheless, being steadily accomplished all the while with the progress of social, political, and commercial intercourse. The greater impulsiveness and vivacity of the French Canadian can brighten up, so to say, the stolidity and ruggedness of the Saxon. The strong common-sense and energy of the Englishman can combine advantageously with the nervous, impetuous activity of the Gaul. Nor should it be forgotten that the French Canadian is not a descendant of the natives of the fickle, sunny South, but that his forefathers came from the more rugged Normandy and Brittany, whose people have much that is akin with the people of the British islands.

In the subsequent portions of this review, the writer will endeavour to follow the progress in culture, not merely of the British-speaking people, but of the two races now working together harmoniously as Canadians. It will not be necessary to dwell at any length on the first period of Canadian history It is quite obvious that in the first centuries of colonial history, but few intellectual fruits can be brought to maturity. In the infancy of a colony or dependency like Canada, whilst men are struggling with the forest and sea for a livelihood, the mass of the people can only find mental food in the utterances of the pulpit, the legislature, and the press. This preliminary chapter would be incomplete were we to forget to bear testimony to the fidelity with which the early Roman Catholic and Protestant missionaries laboured at the great task devolving upon them among the pioneers in the Canadian wilderness. In those times of rude struggle with the difficulties of a colonial life, the religious teachers always threw a gleam of light amid the mental darkness that necessarily prevailed among the toilers of the land

and sea. Bishops Laval, Lartigue, Strachan, and Mountain; Sister Bourgeois, Dr. Burns, Dr. Jas. McGregor, Dr. Anson Green, are conspicuous names among the many religious teachers who did good service in the early times of colonial development. During the first periods of Canadian history, the priest or clergyman was, as often as not, a guide in things temporal as well as spiritual. Dr. Strachan was not simply the instructor in knowledge of many of the Upper Canadian youth who, in after times, were among the foremost men of their day, but was as potent and obstinate in the Council as he was vigorous and decided in the pulpit. When communications were wretched, and churches were the exception, the clergyman was a constant guest in the humble homes of the settlers, who welcomed him as one who not only gave them religious instruction, but on many a winter or autumn evening charmed the listeners in front of the blazing maple logs with anecdotes of the great world of which they too rarely heard. In those early days, the Church of England clergyman was a man generally trained in one of the Universities of the parent state, bringing to the discharge of his duties a conscientious conviction of his great responsibilities, possessing at the same time varied knowledge, and necessarily exercising through his profession and acquirements no inconsiderable influence, not only in a religious but in an intellectual sense as well—an influence which he has never ceased to exercise in this country. It is true as the country became more thickly settled and the people began to claim larger political rights, the influence of many leading minds among the Anglican clergy, who believed in an intimate connection between Church and State, even in a colony, was somewhat antagonistic to the promotion of popular education and the extension of popular government. The Church was too often the Church of the aristocratic and wealthier classes; some of its clergy were sadly wanting in missionary efforts; its magnificent liturgy was too cold and intellectual, perhaps, for the mass: and consequently, in the course of time, the Methodists made rapid progress in Upper Canada. Large numbers of Scotch Presbyterians also settled in the provinces, and exercised a powerful influence on the social, moral and political progress of the country. These pioneers came from a country where parish schools existed long before popular education was dreamed of across the border. Their clergy came from colleges whose course of study cultivated minds of rare analytical and argumentative power. The sermon in the Presbyterian Church is the test of the intellectual calibre of the preacher, whose efforts are followed by his long-headed congregation in a spirit of the keenest criticism, ever ready to detect a want of logic. It is obvious then that the Presbyterian clergyman, from the earliest time he appeared in the history of this country, has always been a considerable force in the mental development of a large section of the people, which has given us, as it will be seen hereafter, many eminent statesmen, journalists, and *litterateurs*.

From the time the people began to have a voice in public affairs, the politician and the journalist commenced naturally to have much influence on the minds of the masses. The labours of the journalist, in connection with the mental development of the country, will be treated at some length in a subsequent part of the review. At present it is sufficient to say that of the different influences that have operated on the minds of the people generally, none has been more important than the Press, notwithstanding the many discouraging circumstances under which it long laboured, in a thinly populated and poor country. The influence of political discussion on the intellect of Canada has been, on the whole, in the direction of expanding the public intelligence, although at times an extreme spirit of partisanship has had the effect of evoking much prejudice and ill-feeling, not calculated to develop the higher attributes of our nature. But whatever may have been the injurious effects of extreme partisanship, the people as a rule have found in the discussion of public matters an excitement which has prevented them from falling into that mental torpor so likely to arise amid the isolation and rude conditions of early times. If the New England States have always been foremost in intellectual movement, it may be attributed in a great measure to the fact that from the first days of their settlement they thought and acted for themselves in all matters of local interest. It was only late in the day when Canadians had an opportunity given them of stimulating their mental faculties by public discussion, but when they were enabled to act for themselves they rapidly improved in mental strength. It is very interesting to Canadians of the present generation to go back to those years when the first Legislatures were opened in the old Bishop's Palace, on the heights of Quebec, and in the more humble structure on the banks of the Niagara River, and study the record of their initiation into parliamentary procedure. It is a noteworthy fact that the French Canadian Legislatures showed from the first an earnest desire to follow, as closely as their circumstances would permit, those admirable rules and principles of procedure which the experience of centuries in England has shown to be necessary to the preservation of decorum, to freedom of speech, and to the protection of the minority. The speeches of the leading men in the two Houses were characterized by evidences of large constitutional knowledge, remarkable for men who had no practical training in parliamentary life. Of course there were in these small Assemblies many men rough in speech and manner, with hardly any education whatever but the writers who refer to them in no very complimentary terms [Footnote: For instance, Talbot, I, chap. 23. He acknowledges, at the same time, the great ability of the leading men, 'who would do credit to the British Parliament.'] always ignore the hardships of their pioneer life, and forget to do justice to their possession, at all events, of good common-sense and much natural acuteness, which enabled them to be of use in their humble way, under the guidance of the few who were in those days the leaders of public opinion. These leaders were generally men drawn from the Bar, who naturally turned to the legislative arena to satisfy their ambition and to cultivate on a larger scale those powers of persuasion and argument in which their professional training naturally made them adepts. With many of these men legislative success was only considered a means of more rapidly attaining the highest honours of their profession, and consequently they were not always the most disinterested guides in the political controversies of the day; but, nevertheless, it must be admitted that, on the whole, the Bar of Canada, then as now, gave the country not a few men who forgot mere selfish considerations, and brought to the discussion of public affairs a wide knowledge and disinterested zeal which showed how men of fine intellect can rise above the narrower range of thought peculiar to continuous practice in the Courts. As public questions became of larger import, the minds of politicians expanded, and enabled them to bring to their discussion a breadth of knowledge and argumentative force which attracted the attention of English statesmen, who were so constantly referred to in those times of our political pupilage, and were by no means too ready to place a high estimate on colonial statesmanship. In the earlier days of our political history some men played so important a part in educating the people to a full comprehension of their political rights that their names must be always gratefully remembered in Canada. Papineau, Bedard, DeValliere, Stuart, Neilson, Baldwin, Lafontaine, Howe, Wilmot, Johnstone, Uniacke, were men of fine intellects—natural-born teachers of the people. Their successors in later times have ably continued the work of perfecting the political structure. All party prejudice aside, every allowance made for political errors in times of violent controversy, the result of their efforts has been not only eminently favourable to the material development of the country but also to the mental vigour of the people. The statesmen who met in council in the ancient city of Quebec during the October of 1864 gave a memorable illustration of their constitutional knowledge and their practical acumen in the famous Resolutions which form the basis of the present Constitution of Canada.

But it is not within the limits of this review to dwell on the political progress of Canada, except so far as it may influence the intellectual development of the people. It will be seen, as we proceed, that the extension of political rights had a remarkable effect in stimulating the public intelligence and especially in improving the mental outfit of the people. The press increased in influence and ability; but, more than all, with the concession of responsible government, education became the great question of the day in the legislatures of the larger provinces. But to so important and interesting a subject it will be necessary to devote a separate chapter.

CHAPTER II.

EDUCATION.

The great educational advantages that the people of Canada now enjoy, and more especially in the premier Province of Ontario — as the splendid exhibit recently made at Paris and Philadelphia has proved to the world — are the results of the legislation of a very few years. A review of the first two periods of our political history affords abundant evidence that there existed in Canada as in Europe much indifference in all matters affecting the general education of the country. Whatever was accomplished during these early times was owing, in a great measure, to the meritorious efforts of ecclesiastical bodies or private individuals. As long as France governed Canada, education was entirely in the hands of the Roman Catholic Church. The Jesuits, Franciscans, and other religious male and female Orders, at an early date, commenced the establishment of those colleges and seminaries which have always had so important a share in the education of Lower Canada. The first school in that province was opened in 1616 at Three Rivers, by Brother Pacifique Duplessis, a Franciscan. The Jesuits founded a College at Quebec in 1831, or three years before the establishment of Harvard and the Ursulines opened their convent in the same city four years later. Sister Bourgeoys, of Troyes, founded at Montreal in 1659 the Congregation de Notre Dame for the education of girls of humble rank, the commencement of an institution which has now its buildings in many parts of Canada. In the latter part of the seventeenth century Mgr. Francois Xavier de Laval-Montmorency, a member of one of the proudest families in Europe, carried out a project of providing education for Canadian priests drawn from the people of the country. Consequently, in addition to the Great Seminary at Quebec, there was the Lesser Seminary where boys were taught in the hope that they would one day take orders. In this project the Indians were included, and several attended when the school was opened in

1668, in the humble dwelling owned by Mme. Couillard, though it was not long before they showed their impatience of scholastic bondage. It is also interesting to learn that, in the inception of education, the French endeavoured in more than one of their institutions to combine industrial pursuits with the ordinary branches of an elementary education. For instance, attached to the Seminary was a sort of farm-school, established in the parish of St. Joachim, below Quebec, the object of which was to train the humbler class of pupils in agricultural as well as certain mechanical pursuits. The manual arts were also taught in the institutions under the charge of the Ursulines and Congregation. We find, for example, a French King giving a thousand francs to a sisterhood of Montreal to buy wool, and the same sum to teach young girls to knit. We also read of the same Sovereign maintaining a teacher of navigation and surveying at Quebec on the modest salary of four hundred francs a-year. But all accounts of the days of the French regime go to show that, despite the zealous efforts of the religious bodies to improve the education of the colonists, secular instruction was at a very low ebb. One writer tells us that 'even the children of officers and gentlemen scarcely knew how to read and write; they were ignorant of the first elements of geography and history.' These were, in fact, days of darkness everywhere, so far as the masses were concerned. Neither England nor France had a system of popular education. Yet it is undoubted that on the whole the inhabitants of Canada had far superior moral and educational advantages than were enjoyed during those times by the mass of people in England and France. Even in the days of Walpole and Hannah More the ignorance of the English peasantry was only equalled by their poverty and moral depravity. [Footnote: Green in his 'History of the English People' says:—Purity and fidelity to the marriage vow were sneered out of fashion; and Lord Chesterfield, in his letters to his son, instructed him in the art of seduction as part of a polite education. At the other end of the social scale lay the masses of the poor. They were ignorant and brutal to a degree which it is hard to conceive, for the vast increase of population which followed on the growth of towns and the development of manufactures had been met by no effort for religious or educational improvement. Not a new parish had been created. Hardly a single new church had been built. Schools there were none save the grammar schools of Edward and Elizabeth. The rural peasantry, who were fast being reduced to pauperism by the poor-laws, were left without moral or religious training of any sort. 'We saw but one bible in the parish of Chedda,' said Hannah More, at a far later time, 'and that was used to prop a flower pot.' p. 707, Harpers' ed. 1870. Parkman also admits that 'towards the end of the French regime the Canadian habitant was probably better taught, so far as concerned religion, than the mass of French peasants.'—*The Old Regime in Canada.*]

Sensuality was not encouraged in Canada by the leaders of society, as was notoriously the case in the best circles of England and of France. Dull and devoid of intellectual light as was the life of the Canadian, he had his places of worship, where he had a moral training which elevated him immeasurably above the peasantry of England as well as of his old home. The clergy of Lower Canada confessedly did their best to relieve the ignorance of the people, but they were naturally unable to accomplish, by themselves, a task which properly devolved on the governing class. But under the French regime in Canada, the civil authorities were as little anxious to enlighten the people by the establishment of schools as they were to give them a voice in the government of the country. In remarkable contrast with the conduct of the French Government in this particular were the efforts of the Puritan pioneers then engaged in the work of civilization among the rocks of New England. Learning, after religion and social order, was the object nearest to the hearts of the New England fathers; or rather it may be said that they were convinced that social order and a religious character could not subsist in the absence of mental culture. As early as 1647, Governor Winthrop sanctioned a measure [Footnote: This measure provided that 'every township in this jurisdiction, after the Lord has increased them to the number of 50 householders, shall then forthwith appoint one within their town, to teach all such children as shall resort to him, to write and read, whose wages shall be paid, either by the parents or masters of such children, or by the inhabitants in general, by way of supply.' And it was further ordered that 'when any town shall increase to the number of one hundred families, or householders, they shall set up a grammar school, the master thereof being able to instruct youth so far as they may be fitted for the University.'] which was the first school law ever passed in America, and outlined just such a system as we now enjoy on an extended scale in Canada. Wise men those stern Puritans of the early colonial times! It is not surprising that intellectual food, so early provided for all classes, should have nurtured at last an Emerson, an Everett, a Hawthorne, a Wendell Philips, a Longfellow, a Lowell, a Howells, and a Parkman.

After the Conquest the education of the people made but little progress in Lower Canada. Education was confined for the most part to the Quebec Seminary, and a few other institutions under the control of religious communities, permitted to remain in the country. Lord Dorchester appointed a Commission in 1787, to enquire into the whole subject, but no practical results followed the step. In 1792 the Duke de Rochefoucauld wrote that 'the Canadian who could read was regarded as a phenomenon.' The attempt of the 'Royal Institution for the Advancement of Learning' to establish schools was comparatively a failure; for after an existence of twenty years it had only 37 schools, attended by 1,048 pupils altogether. The British Government, at no time after it came into possession of the province, ever attempted anything for the promotion of general education. Indeed, the only matter in which it appeared in connection with education was one by no means creditable to it; for it applied the Jesuits' estates, which were destined for education, to a species of fund for secret service, and for a number of years maintained an obstinate struggle with the Assembly in order to continue this misappropriation. No doubt the existing antagonism of races, then so great an evil in Lower Canada, prevented anything like co-operation in this matter; but added to this was, probably, a doubt among the ruling class in Canada, as in England, as to the wisdom of educating the masses. An educational report of 1824 informs us that 'generally not above one-fourth of the entire population could read, and not above one-tenth of them could write even imperfectly.' In the presentments of the grand juries, and in the petitions on public grievances so frequently presented to Parliament, the majority of the signers were obliged to make their marks. During the year 1824, the Fabrique Act was passed with the view of relieving the public ignorance, but unhappily the political difficulties that prevailed from that time prevented any effective measures being carried out for the establishment of public schools throughout the province.

Nor was education in the western province in a much better state during the first period of Parliamentary Government, that is from 1792 to 1840. It is noteworthy, however, that high schools for the education of the wealthier classes were established at a very early date in the province. The first classical school was opened in the old town of Kingston by the Rev. Dr. Stuart. In 1807 the first Education Act was passed, establishing grammar schools in each of the eight districts in which the province was divided, and endowing them with an annual stipend of one hundred pounds each. In 1816 the first steps were taken by the Legislature in the direction of common schools—as they were then, and for some time afterwards, desig-nated—but the Acts that were then and subsequently passed up to the time of the Union were very inadequate to accomplish the object aimed at. No general system existed; the masters were very inferior and ill paid. A very considerable portion of the province was with-out schools as well as churches. Of the lands which were generally appropriated to the support of the former by far the most valuable portion was diverted to the endowment of King's College. In 1838 there were 24,000 children in the common schools, out of a popula-tion of 450,000, leaving probably some 50,000 destitute of the means of education. The well-to-do classes, however, especially those liv-ing in the large towns, had good opportunities of acquiring a sound education. Toronto was well supplied with establishments, sup-ported by large endowments: Upper Canada College, the Home District Grammar School, besides some well conducted seminaries for young ladies. For years Cornwall Grammar School, under the superintendence of the energetic Dr. Strachan was the resort of the provincial aristocracy. Among the men who received their early education in that famous establishment were Robert Baldwin, H. J. Boulton, J. B. Macaulay, Allan McNab, John Beverley Robinson, Dean Bethune, Clark Gamble, and many others afterwards famous in politics, in law and in the church. Dr. Strachan was not only a sound scholar but an astute man of the world, admirably fitted to develop the talents of his pupils and prepare them for the active duties of life in those young days of Canada. 'In conducting your education,' said he on one occasion, 'one of my principal duties has always been to fit you for discharging with credit the duties of any office to which you may hereafter be called. To accomplish this it was necessary for you to be accustomed frequently to depend upon and think for yourselves. Accordingly, I have always encouraged this disposition, which, when preserved within due bounds, is one of the greatest benefits that can possibly be acquired. To enable you to think with advantage, I not only regulated your tasks in such a manner as to exercise your judgment, but extended them for you beyond the mechanical routine of study usually adopted in schools.' [Footnote: Scadding's 'Toronto of Old,' p. 161.] None of the masters of the high schools of the present day could do as much under the very scientific system which limits their freedom of action in the educational training of their scholars. But whilst the wealthier classes in the larger centres of population could avail themselves of the services of such able teachers as the late Bishop of Toronto, the mass of people were left in a state of ignorance. The good schools were controlled by clergymen of the different denominations; in fact, the Church of England was nearly dominant in such matters in those early times, and it must be admitted that there was a spirit abroad in the province which discredited all attempts to place the education of the masses on a more liberal basis.

The Union of 1840 and the extension of the political rights of the people gave a new impulse to useful and practical legislation in a country whose population commenced from that time to increase very rapidly. In 1841, 1843 and 1844 measures were passed for the improvement of the school system of both provinces. In 1846, the system of compulsory taxation for the support of public schools was, for the first time, embodied in the law, and education at last made steady progress. According as experience showed the necessity of changes, the Legislature improved the educational system of both provinces—these changes having been continued to be made since Confederation. In Lower Canada, the names of two men will always be honourably associated with the working out of the School Law, and these are Dr. Meilleur and Hon. Mr. Chauveau, the latter of whom succeeded in establishing Normal Schools at Montreal and Quebec. In the Province of Ontario, Egerton Ryerson has perpetuated his name from one end of the country to the other, where the young are being educated in large, comfortable school-houses by a class of teachers whose qualifications, on the whole, are of a high order.

Great as has been the progress of education in Quebec, yet it must be admitted that it is in some respects behind that of Ontario. The buildings are inferior, the teachers less efficient, and insufficiently paid in many cases—and efficiency, no doubt, depends in a great measure on the remuneration. The ratio of children who are ignorant of the elements of knowledge is greater than in the Province of Ontario, where, it must be remembered, there is more wealth and, perhaps, more ambition among the people generally. Still the tendency in Quebec is in the direction of progress, and as the people become better off, they will doubtless be induced to work out their system, on the whole so admirable, with greater zeal and energy.

In the Province of Ontario every child can receive a free education, and can pass from the Public School to the High School or Collegiate Institute, and thence to the University, where the fees are small and many scholarships are offered to the industrious student. The principles which lie at the basis of the system are local assessment to supplement State aid; thorough inspection of all schools; ensuring the best teachers by means of Normal Schools and competitive examinations, complete equipment, graded examinations, and separate schools. The State recognises its obligation to the child, not only by contributing pecuniary aid, but by exercising a general supervision, by means of a Superintendent in Quebec and by a Minister of the Crown in Ontario. The system of Ontario, which has been the prototype for the legislation of all the smaller provinces, is eclectic, for it is the result of a careful examination of the systems that prevail in the United States, Prussia, and Ireland.

As in the larger provinces, much apathy was shown in Nova Scotia for many years on the subject of the education of the people. Unhappily this apathy lasted much longer; for the census of 1861 proved that out of a population of 284,000 persons over five years of age, no less than 81,469 could not read a printed page, and 114,877 could not write their names. It was not till 1864 that Sir Charles Tupper, then Premier, brought in a comprehensive measure containing the best features of the Ontario system; and the result has been a remarkable development in the education of the province. In

New Brunswick, where the public schools were long in a very inferior state—though parish schools had been established as early as 1823—the system was remodelled, in 1871, on that of Ontario, though no provision was made for Separate Schools—an omission which has created much bitterness in the province, as the political history of Canada for the subsequent years abundantly testifies. In Prince Edward Island the first free schools were established in 1852, and further improvements have been made of recent years. In British Columbia, the Legislature has adopted substantially the Ontario School Law with such modifications as are essential to the different circumstances of a sparse population. In the North-west, before the formation of the Province of Manitoba, education was in a much better condition than the isolation and scattered state of the population would have led one to expect. In 1857 there were seventeen schools in the settlements, generally under the supervision of the clergy of the Roman Catholic, Episcopalian, and Presbyterian bodies. In the Collegiate School, managed by the Church of England, and supported, like all other institutions in the country, by contributions from abroad, Aeschylus, Herodotus, Thucydides and Livy were read with other classics besides mathematics. In 1871 a school law of a liberal character was passed, provision being made for Protestant and Roman Catholic schools separately.

The higher branches of education have been taught from a very early date in the history of all the provinces. In the Jesuit College, the Quebec Seminary, and other Roman Catholic institutions founded in Montreal, St. Hyacinthe, Three Rivers, and Nicolet, young men could always be educated for the priesthood, or receive such higher education as was considered necessary in those early times. The Quebec Seminary always occupied a foremost position as an educational institution of the higher order, and did much to foster a love for learning among those classes who were able to enjoy the advantages it offered them. [Footnote: Mr. Buller, in his Educational Report to Lord Durham, says: 'I spent some hours in the experimental lecture-room of the eminent Professor M. Casault, and I think that I saw there the best and most extensive set of philosophic apparatus which is yet to be found in the Colonies of British North America. The buildings are extensive, and its chambers airy and clean; it has a valuable library, and a host of professors and masters.

It secures to the student an extensive course of education.'] It has already been noticed that a Grammar School system was established in the years of the first settlement of Ontario. Governor Simcoe first suggested the idea of a Provincial University, and valuable lands were granted by George III., in 1798, for that purpose. The University of Toronto, or King's College, as it was first called, was established originally under the auspices of the Church of England, and was endowed in 1828, but it was not inaugurated and opened until 1843. Upper Canada College, intended as a feeder to the University, dates back as far as the same time, when it opened with a powerful array of teachers, drawn for the most part from Cambridge. In 1834, the Wesleyan Methodists laid the foundation of Victoria College, at Cobourg, and it was incorporated in 1841, as a University, with the well-known Rev. Dr. Ryerson as its first President. The Kirk of Scotland established Queen's College, at Kingston, in 1841, and the Presbyterian Church of Canada, Knox's College, at Toronto, in 1844. The Roman Catholics founded Regiopolis, at Kingston, in 1846; St. Joseph's College, at Ottawa, in 1846; St Michael's, at Toronto, in 1852. Trinity College, under the auspices of the Church of England, was the issue of the successful effort that was made, in 1849, to throw King's College open to all denominations. Bishop Strachan determined never to lend his countenance to what he called 'a Godless University,' and succeeded in founding an institution which has always occupied a creditable position among the higher educational establishments of the country. The Baptists established the Woodstock Literary Institute in 1857; the Episcopal Methodists, Albert College, at Belleville, in 1866; and the Evangelical section of the Church of England, in 1878, obtained a charter for Huron College, under the name of the Western University of London.

But the great Province of Ontario cannot lay claim to the honour of having established the first Colleges with University powers in British North America. King's College at Windsor, in Nova Scotia — the old home of 'Sam Slick' — was the first institution of a high order founded in the provinces, its history as an academy going as far back as 1788, when Upper Canada had no government of its own. This institution has always remained under the control of the Church of England, and continues to hold a respectable position among educational institutions. Dalhousie College was established at Halifax in 1820, chiefly through the efforts of the Presbyterian Church. In 1831 the Baptists founded Acadia in Horton, and in 1843 the Wesleyans an Academy at Sackville, N. B.—a neutral ground as it were—which was afterwards elevated to the dignity of a University. The Catholics founded St. Mary's at Halifax in 1840, and St Francois Xavier at Antigonishe in 1855. In 1876 the experiment was commenced, at Halifax, of a University to hold examinations in arts, law, and medicine, and to confer degrees. In New Brunswick, King's College was established at Fredericton in 1828 under the control of the Church of England, but in 1858 it was made non-sectarian under the designation of the University of New Brunswick. Even the little Provinces of Prince Edward Island and Manitoba have aspirations in the same way, for the University of Manitoba was established a year or two ago, and the Prince of Wales College followed the visit of His Royal Highness to Charlottetown in 1860.

The establishment of Laval University was an important event in the annals of education of the Province of Quebec. Bishop Bourget of Montreal first suggested the idea of interesting the Quebec Seminary in the project. The result was the visit of the Principal, M. Louis Casault, to Europe, where he obtained a Royal charter, and studied the best university systems. The charter was signed in 1852, and the Pope approved the scheme, and authorized the erection of chairs of theology and the conferring of degrees. The University of McGill is an older institution than Laval. The noble bequest to which it owes its origin was for many years a source of expensive litigation, and it was not till 1821 that it received a charter, and only in 1829 was it able to commence operations. In fact, it cannot be said to have made any substantial progress till 1854, when it was re-organized with a distinguished Nova Scotian scientist as its Principal—Dr. J. W. Dawson—to whom his native province previously owed much for his efforts to improve education at a time when it was in a very low state, owing to the apathy of the Legislature. Bishop's College at Lennoxville was established in 1844, for the education of members of the Church of England, through the exertions of Bishop Mountain, but it was not till 1853 that it was erected into a University. Besides these institutions, the Roman Catholics and other denominations have various colleges and academies at different important points—such as St. Hyacinthe, Montreal, Masson and L'Assomption Colleges. The Government of the Dominion have also established, at Kingston, an institution where young men may receive a training to fit them for the military profession—an institution something on the model of West Point—the practical benefits of which, however, are not as yet appreciable in a country like this, which has no regular army, and cannot afford employment suitable for the peculiar studies necessarily followed in the Academy. The Ontario Government are also trying the experiment, on an expensive scale, of teaching young men agriculture, practically and scientifically—a repetition, under more favourable circumstances, of what was tried centuries ago by the religious communities of Quebec. Nor, in reviewing the means of mental equipment in Canada, must we forget the many establishments which are now provided for the education of young women outside of the Public and High Schools, the most notable being the Roman Catholic Convents of Notre Dame and Sacre Coeur, Ottawa Ladies' College, Wesleyan Ladies' College at Hamilton, Brantford Ladies' College, Bishop Strachan School at Toronto, Helmuth Ladies' College at London, Albert College, and Woodstock Literary Institute, besides many minor institutions of more or less merit. Several of our universities have also shown a liberal progressive spirit in acknowledging the right of women to participate in the higher education, hitherto confined to men in this country—an illustration in itself of the intellectual development that is now going on among us.

When we proceed to review the statistics of educational progress, they present very gratifying results. The following table, carefully prepared to the latest date, from the voluminous official returns annually presented to the different Legislatures of the Provinces of Canada, will be quite sufficient for the purposes of this paper:

Total number of public educational institutions in the Dominion 13,800

Number of pupils in attendance throughout the year 925,000
Amount now annually contributed by the State and People $6,700,000

Number of Colleges and Universities 21
Number of Undergraduates in Arts, Law, Medicine, Theology,
about 2,200

Number of Superior and High Schools, including Academies and
    Collegiate Institutes 443
Aggregate attendance in same 141,000

Number of Normal Schools 8
Number of students in same 1,400

Amount expended in Ontario alone during 30 years (from 1850 to 1880,) for erection and repairs of School-houses, fuel and contingencies, about $15,000,000

[Footnote: The educational statistics preceding 1850 are not easily ascertained, and in any case are small. I have not been able to obtain similar figures for other provinces; in fact, in some cases, they are not to be ascertained with any degree of accuracy.]

Total amount expended in same province, for all educational purposes during same period, upwards of $50,000,000

Total amount (approximate), available for public school purposes, in *all* Canada, since Confederation, *i.e.* in 12 years $64,000,000

These statistics prove conclusively, that Canada occupies a foremost position among communities for its zeal in developing the education of the people, irrespective of class. The progress that has been made within forty years may be also illustrated by the fact that, in 1839, there were in all the public and private schools of British North America only some 92,000 young people, out of a total population of 1,440,000, or about one in fifteen, whilst now the proportion may be given at one in four, if we include the students in all educational institutions. But it must be admitted, that it is to Ontario we must look for illustrations of the most perfect educational system. There, from the very commencement, the admirable municipal system which was one of the best results of the Union of 1840, enabled the people to prove their public spirit by carrying out with great energy the different measures passed by the Legislature for the promotion of Public Schools. 'By their constitution, the municipal and school corporations are reflections of the sentiments and feelings of the people within their respective circles of jurisdiction; their powers are adequate to meet all the economic exigencies of each municipality, whether of schools or roads, of the diffusion of knowledge, or the development of wealth.' [Footnote: Hon. Adam Crooks, Minister of Education, Report on Educational Institutions of Ontario, for Philadelphia Exhibition, p. 45.] As a result of such public spirit, we find in Ontario the finest specimens of school architecture, and the most perfect school apparatus and appliances of every kind, calculated to assist the teacher and pupil, and to bring into play their best mental faculties. But there can be no doubt that the success of the system rests in a very great measure on the effort that has been made to improve the status of the teacher. The schoolmaster is no longer a man who resorts to education because everything else has failed. He is no longer one of that class of 'adventurers, many of them persons of the lowest grade,' who, we are told, infested the rural districts of Upper Canada in olden times, 'wheresoever they found the field unoccupied; pursuing their speculation with pecuniary profit to themselves, but with certainly little advantage to the moral discipline of their youthful pupils.' [Footnote: Preston's 'Three Years in Canada' (1837-9), p. 110, Vol. ii.] The fact that such men could be instructors of youth, half a century ago, is of itself a forcible illustration of the public indifference to the question of popular education. All the legislation in Ontario, and in the other provinces as well, has been framed with the object of elevating the moral and intellectual standing of a class on whose efforts so much of the future happiness and prosperity of this country depends. On the whole, the object has been successfully achieved, and the schoolmasters of Ontario are, as a rule, a superior class of men. Yet it must be admitted that much can still be done to improve their position. Education, we all know, does not necessarily bring with it refinement; that can only come by constant communication with a cultured society, which is not always, in Canada, ready to admit the teacher on equal terms. It may also be urged that the teacher, under the system as now perfected, is far too much of an automaton—a mere machine, wound up to proceed so far and no farther. He is not allowed sufficient of that free volition which would enable him to develop the best qualities of his pupils, and to elevate their general tone. Polite manners among the pupils are just as valuable as orderly habits. Teachers cannot strive too much to check all rudeness among the youth, many of whom have few opportunities to cultivate those social amenities which make life so pleasant, and also do so much to soften the difficulties of one's journey through life. [Footnote: Since the above was written, I find the following remarks by Mr. Adam, editor of the *Canada Educational Monthly*, to the same purport: 'The tone of the Schools might be largely raised and the tender and plastic nature of the young minds under training be directed into sympathy with the noble and the elevating. Relieved of much of the red-tapism which hampers the work of the High-School teacher, the masters of the Public Schools have more opportunity to make individuality tell in the conduct of the school, and of encircling the sphere of their work with a bright zone of cultivation and refinement. But the Public School teacher will accomplish much if, reverently and sympathetically, he endeavours to preserve the freshness and ingenuousness of childhood and, by the influence of his own example, while leading the pupil up the golden ladder of mental acquisition, he encourages the cultivation of those graces of life which are the best adornments of youth.'—Feb. 1879.] Such discipline cannot be too rigidly followed in a country of a Saxon race, whose *brusquerie* of manner and speech is a natural heritage, just as a spirit of courtesy seems innate in the humblest *habitants* who have not yet forgotten, among the rude conditions of their American life, that prominent characteristic of a Gallic people. [Footnote: More than forty years ago, Mr. Buller, in his report to Lord Durham on the State of Education in Lower Canada, pays this tribute to the peasantry: 'Withal this is a people eminently qualified to reap advantages from education; they are shrewd and intelligent, never morose, most amiable in their domestic relations, and *most graceful in their manners*.']

It is quite probable that the Public School system of this country is still defective in certain respects, which can only be satisfactorily improved with the progress of experience. The remarks of a writer in a recent number of a popular American magazine, *Scribner's Monthly*, may have some application to ourselves, when he says that there is now-a-days 'too decided an aim to train everybody to pass an examination in everything;' that the present system 'encourages two virtues — to forgive and forget, in time to forgive the examiner, and to forget the subject of the examination.' The present writer does not wish — in fact, it is rather beyond the limit he has marked out for this review — to go into any lengthy discussion of matters which are worthy, however, of consideration by all those interested in perfecting the details of the educational system in Ontario; but he may refer, *en passant,* to the somewhat remarkable multiplication of text-books, many of which are carelessly got up, simply to gratify the vanity and fill the purse of some educationist, anxious to get into print. Grammar also appears to be a lost art in the Public Schools, where the students are perplexed by books, not simple, but most complex in their teachings, calculated to bewilder persons of mature analytical minds, and to make one appreciate more highly than ever the intelligible lessons of Lennie's homely little volume, which was the favourite in those times when education was not quite so much reduced to a science. But these are, after all, only among the details which can be best treated by teachers themselves, in those little parliaments which have grown up of recent years, and where educationists have admirable opportunities of comparing their experiences, and suggesting such improvements as may assist in the intellectual development of the young, and at the same time elevate their own social standing in this country. On the whole, Canada has much reason for congratulation in possessing a system which brings education in every province within the reach of all, and enables a lad to cultivate his intellectual faculties to a point sufficient to place him in the years of his mature manhood in the highest position that this country offers to its sons. As to the objection, not unfrequently urged, that the tendency of the public school education of this country is to withdraw the young from the industrial avocations of life, it may be forcibly met by the fact, that it is to the New England States we look for the best evidences of industrial, as well as intellectual, development. The looms of Massachusetts and Connecticut are not less busy — the inventive genius of those States is not less fertile, because their public schools are teeming with their youth. But it is not necessary to go to the neighbouring

States to give additional force to these remarks; for in no part of the Dominion, is there so much industrial energy as in the Province of Ontario, where the school system is the best. An English gentleman, who has devoted more attention than the majority of his country-men to the study of colonial subjects, has well observed on this point: 'A key to one of the principal causes of their successful pro-gress in the development of industrial art is probably to be found in their excellent and superior educational system.' [Footnote: Address of Mr. Frederick Young on the Paris Exhibition, before the Royal Colonial Institute, 1878-9.]

A review of the University system of this country, on the perfec-tion of which depends the higher culture of the people, shows us that the tendency continues to be in the direction of strengthening the denominational institutions. The Universities of Toronto and McGill are the principal non-sectarian institutions of a higher class, which appear to be on a popular and substantial basis. It is natural enough that each denomination should rally around a college, which rests on a religious basis. Parents seem in not a few cases to appreciate very highly the moral security that the denominational system appears to afford to their sons—a moral security which they believe to be wanting in the case of non-sectarian institutions. Even those colleges which do not shut their doors to young men of any particular creed continue to be more or less supported by the de-nominations under whose auspices they were first established. No doubt, these colleges, sufficiently numerous for a sparsely peopled country like Canada, are doing a valuable work in developing the intellectual faculties of the youth of the several provinces. It is a question, however, if the perpetuation of a system which multiplies colleges with University powers in each province, will tend to pro-duce the soundest scholarship in the end. What we want even now are not so many 'Admirable Crichtons' with a smattering of all sorts of knowledge, but men recognised for their proficiency in special branches of learning. Where there is much competition, there must be sooner or later an inclination to lower the standard, and degrade the value of the diplomas issued at the close of a college course. Theoretically, it seems preferable that in a great province like Ontar-io, the diplomas should emanate from one Central University au-thority rather than from a number of colleges, each pursuing its own curriculum. No doubt it is also quite possible to improve our higher system of education so as to make it more in conformity with the practical necessities of the country. An earnest discussion has been going on for some time in the United States as to the inferiority of the American University System compared with that of Germany. [Footnote: An article, in the July number of *Harper's* for 1880, by so distinguished an authority as Professor Draper, is well worthy of perusal by those who wish to pursue this subject at greater length. Among other things he says (pp. 253-4): 'There is therefore in America a want of a school offering opportunities to large and constantly increasing classes of men for pursuing professional studies—a want which is deeply felt, and which sends every year many students and millions of dollars out of the country. Where in the United States can a young man prepare himself thoroughly to become a teacher of the ancient classics. A simple college course is not enough. The Germans require that their teachers of Latin and Greek should pursue the classics as a specialty for three years at a University after having completed the gymnasium which, as a classical school, would be universally admitted to rank with our colleges.... If an American (or a Canadian) wishes to pursue a special course in history, politics and political economy, mathematics, philosophy, or in any one of many other studies lying outside of the three professions, law, medicine, and theology, he must go to Europe. Again, whoever desires even in theology, law and medicine to select from one branch as a specialty, must go to Europe to do so.' Hon. Mr. Blake, in his last address as Chancellor of Toronto University, also dwelt very forcibly on the necessity of *post graduate* courses of study in special subjects.—*Canada Educational Monthly*, Oct. 1880.] John-Hopkins University in Baltimore, Michigan University, and Cornell University, are illustrations of the desire to enlarge the sphere of the education of the people. If we had the German system in this country, men could study classics or mathematics, or science, or literature, or law, or medicine, in a national University with a sole view to their future avocations in life. It is true, in the case of law and medicine Laval, Toronto, McGill and other Universities in the provinces have organized professional courses; and there is no doubt a desire on the part of the educational authorities in these institutions to ensure proficiency so far as the comparatively limited means at their command permit them. It is certainly a noteworthy fact—lately pointed out by Mr. Blake—that during the last five years only one fourth of the entrants into Osgoode Hall were graduates of any University, and three-fourths were men who had taken no degree, and yet there is no profession which demands a higher mental training than the Bar. In medical education there is certainly less laxity than in the United States; all the efforts of medical men being laudably directed to lengthen the course and develop the professional knowledge of the students. Still, not a few of our young men show their appreciation of the need of even a wider knowledge and experience than is afforded in the necessarily limited field of Canadian study, by spending some time in the great schools and hospitals of Europe. Of course, in a new country, where there is a general desire to get to the practical work of life with as little delay as possible, the tendency to be carefully guarded against is the giving too large facilities to enter professions where life and property are every day at stake. It is satisfactory, however, to know that the tendency in Canada is rather in the other direction, and that an institution like McGill College, which is a Medical College of high reputation, is doing its best with the materials at command, to perfect the medical knowledge of those who seek its generous aid. No doubt the time is fast approaching when the State will be obliged to give greater assistance to Toronto University so as to enable it to enter on a broader and more liberal system of culture, commensurate with the development of science and literature. Unless the State makes a liberal effort in this direction, we are afraid it will be some time before University College will be in a position to imitate the praiseworthy example set by Columbia College, which, from its situation in the great commercial metropolis, and the large means at its command, seems likely to be the great American University of the future. It must be remembered that the intellectual requirements of the Dominion must continue to increase with great rapidity, since there is greater wealth accumulating, and a praiseworthy ambition for higher culture. The legislature and the public service are making very heavy requisitions on the intellect of this much governed country, with its numerous Parliaments and Cabinets and large body of officials, very many of whom are entrusted with the most responsible duties, demanding no ordinary mental qualifications. [Footnote: It is a fact worthy of mention in this connection, that in the English House of Commons dissolved in 1880, 236, or more than a third out of 658, members were Oxford or Cambridge men, while about 180 were 'public school men,'—the 'public schools' being Eton and such high class institutions. In a previous English Cabinet, the majority were Honor men; Mr. Gladstone is a double first of Christ Church, Oxford.]

The public schools, collegiate institutes, and universities, apart from the learned professions, must also every year make larger demands on the intellectual funds of the Dominion, and as the remuneration of the masters and professors in the educational institutions of this country should in the nature of things improve in the future, our young men must be necessarily stimulated to consider such positions more worthy of a life's devotion. Under such circumstances, it should be the great object of all true friends of the sound intellectual development of Canada to place our system of higher education on a basis equal to the exigencies of a practical, prescient age, and no longer cling to worn out ideas of the past. In order to do this, let the people of Ontario determine to establish a national University which will be worthy of their great province and of the whole Dominion. Toronto University seems to have in some measure around it that aroma of learning, that dignity of age, and that prestige of historic association which are necessary to the successful establishment of a national seat of learning, and will give the fullest scope to Canadian talent.

CHAPTER III.

JOURNALISM.

In the development of Canadian intellect the newspaper press has had a very large influence during the past half-century and more. What the pulpit has done for the moral education of the people, the press has accomplished for their general culture when schools were few and very inferior, and books were rarely seen throughout the country. When the political rights of the people were the subject of earnest controversy in the Legislatures of the Provinces the press enabled all classes to discuss public questions with more or less knowledge, and gave a decided intellectual stimulus, which had a valuable effect in a young isolated country like Canada. In the days of the French *regime* there was not a single printing press in Canada, though the *News Letter* was published in Boston as early as 1704. [Footnote: The first printing press in America wag set up at Cambridge, in the ninth year of the Charter Government (1639); the first document printed was the 'Freeman's Oath,' then an almanack, and next the Psalms.—2 Palgrave, 45. In 1740, there were no less than eleven journals—only of foolscap size, however—published in the English Colonies.] It is generally claimed that the first newspaper in Canada, was the Quebec *Gazette*, which was published in 1764, by Brown & Gilmour, formerly Philadelphia printers, with a subscription list of only one hundred and fifty names. The first issue appeared on the 21st June, printed on four folio pages of 18 by 12 inches, each containing two columns of small type. The first article was the prospectus in larger type, in which the promoters promised to pay particular attention 'to the refined amusements of literature and the pleasant veins of well-pointed wit; interspersed with chosen pieces of curious essays, extracted from the most celebrated authors, blending philosophy with politics, history, &c.' The conductors also pledged themselves to give no place in the paper to 'party prejudices and private scandal'—a pledge better kept than such promises are generally. There was a very slender allowance of news from Riga, St. Petersburg, London, New York and Philadelphia; but there was one ominous item, that Parliament was about imposing taxes on the Colonies, though they were without representation in that Parliament. The latest English news was to the 11th April; the latest American to the 7th May. Only two advertisements appeared—one of a general store, of dry goods, groceries, hardware, all the *olla podrida* necessary in those days; the other from the Honourable Commissioner of Customs, warning the public against making compositions for duties under the Imperial Act. This sheet, for some years, had no influence on public opinion; for it continued to be a mere bald summary of news, without comment on political events. Indeed, when it was first issued, the time was unfavourable for political discussion, as Quebec had only just become an English possession, and the whole country was lying torpid under the military administration of General Murray. It is, however, a fact not very generally known even yet, except to a few antiquarians, that there was a small sheet published in British America, called the Halifax *Gazette* [Footnote: In a letter of Secretary Cotterell, written in 1754, to Captain Floyer, at Piziquid (Windsor), he refers to M. Dandin, a priest in one of the Acadian settlements: 'If he chooses to play *bel esprit* in the Halifax *Gazette*, he may communicate his matter to the printer as soon as he pleases, as he will not print it without showing it to me.—See Murdoch's History of Nova Scotia, vol. 2, p. 234] just twelve years before the appearance of the Quebec paper. From 1769 we commence to find regular mention of the Nova Scotia *Gazette and Weekly Chronicle*, published on Sackville Street by A. Fleury, who also printed the first Almanac in Canada, in 1774. One of the first newspapers published in the Maritime Provinces was the *Royal Gazette and New Brunswick Advertiser*, which appeared in 1785 in St. John, just founded by the American Loyalists. The first paper appeared in Upper Canada on the establishment of Parliamentary Government, and was published by Louis Roy, at Newark, on the 18th April, 1793, under the title of *The Upper Canada Gazette, or the American Oracle*. The sheet was in folio, 15 by 9-1/2 inches, of coarse, but durable paper—not a characteristic, certainly, of our great newspapers now-a-days, of which the material is very flimsy; the impression was fairly executed; the price was three dollars a year. In 1794, the form was changed to a quarto, and one Tiffany had become the proprietor. When the *Gazette* was removed to York, in 1800, with all the Government offices, the Messrs. Tiffany started the *Constellation*, which, Dr. Scadding tells us, illustrated the jealousy which the people of the Niagara district felt at seeing York suddenly assume so much importance; for one of the writers ironically proposes a 'Stump Act' for the ambitious, though muddy, unkempt little town, 'so that the people in the space of a few months, may relapse into intoxication with impunity, and stagger home at any hour of the night without encountering the dreadful apprehension of broken necks.'

The *Constellation* only lived a year or two, and then gave way to the *Herald* and other papers at subsequent dates; and it is an interesting fact, mentioned by the learned antiquarian of Toronto, that the imposing stone used by Mr. Tiffany, was in use up to 1870, when the old *Niagara Mail*, long edited by Mr. W. Kirby, at last ceased publication. The *Gazette* and *Oracle* continued to be published at York by different printers, and, like other journals in America, often appeared in variegated colours—blue being the favourite—in consequence of the scarcity of white paper. The title, *American Oracle*, was dropped from the heading when Dr. Horne became the publisher, in 1817; it continued to publish official notices, besides meagre summaries of general news, and some miscellaneous reading matter.

The second paper in Upper Canada was the *Upper Canada Guardian* or *Freeman's Journal*, which was edited and printed by Joseph Willcox, who fell under the ban of the Lieutenant Governor, for his Liberal opinions. It was printed in 1807, and exercised much influence for a time as an organ of the struggling Liberal party. Like others, in those days of political bitterness, its editor was imprisoned, ostensibly for a breach of parliamentary privilege, though in reality as a punishment for presuming to differ from the governing party; but, able man as he undoubtedly was, he marred his career by an infamous desertion to the Americans during the war of 1812, before the expiration of which he was killed. The first newspaper in Kingston, the third in the province, was the *Gazette*, founded in 1810, by Stephen Miles, who afterwards became a minister of the Methodist denomination, and also printed the Grenville *Gazette*, the first journal in the old town of Prescott. [Footnote: Morgan's 'Bibliotheca Canadensis,' Art. Miles.] The first daily paper published in British North America, appears to have been the *Daily Advertiser*, which appeared in Montreal, in May, 1833—the *Herald* and *Gazette* being tri-weekly papers at the time. The *Daily Advertiser* was issued in the interests of the Liberals, under the management of the Hon. H. S. Chapman, subsequently a judge in New Zealand. One of the chief inducements held out to subscribers was the regular publication of full prices current and other commercial information. The *British Whig*, of Kingston, was the first newspaper that attempted the experiment of a daily issue in Upper Canada.

It is a noteworthy fact, which can be best mentioned here, that the first newspaper in Three Rivers was the *Gazette*, published by one Stobbs, in 1832, more than two centuries after the settlement of that town, which has always been in the midst of the most thickly settled district of Lower Canada. At that time, newspapers were rapidly gaining ground in Upper Canada—districts not so old by months or weeks even as Three Rivers had years, and with a more scattered population, not exceeding one-fifth of that of the Three Rivers district, could boast of, at least, one newspaper. [Footnote: Quebec *Mercury*, 1832.]

In 1827, Mr. Jotham Blanchard, the ancestor of a well-known family of
Liberals in the Lower Provinces, established the first newspaper outside
of Halifax, the *Colonial Patriot*, at Pictou, a flourishing town on the Straits of Northumberland, chiefly settled by the Scotch.

In 1839, Mr. G. Fenety—now 'Queen's Printer' at Fredericton — established the *Commercial News*, at St. John, New Brunswick, the first tri-weekly and penny paper in the Maritime Provinces, which he conducted for a quarter of a century, until he disposed of it to Mr. Edward Willis, under whose editorial supervision it has always exercised considerable influence in the public affairs of the province. The first daily paper published in the Province of Nova Scotia, was the Halifax *Morning Post*, appearing in 1845, edited by John H. Crosskill but it had a brief existence, and tri-weeklies continued to be published for many years—the old *Colonist* representing the

Conservatives, and the *Chronicle* the Liberals, of the province. The senior of the press, in the Lower Provinces, however, is the *Acadian Recorder*, the first number of which appeared in 1813.

The only mention I have been able to find of a newspaper in the brief histories of Prince Edward Island, is of the appearance, in 1823, of the *Register*, printed and edited by J. D. Haszard, who distinguished himself at the outset of his career by a libel on one of the Courts before which he was summoned with legal promptitude—just as printers are now-a-days in Manitoba—and dismissed with a solemn reprimand, on condition of revealing the authors of the libel. The remarks of the Chancellor (who appears to have been also the Governor of the Island), in dismissing the culprit, are quite unique in their way. 'I compassionate your youth and inexperience; did I not do so, I would lay you by the heels long enough for you to remember it. You have delivered your evidence fairly, plainly and clearly, and as became a man; but I caution you, when you publish anything again, keep clear, Sir, of a Chancellor. Beware, Sir, of a Chancellor.' [Footnote: Campbell's Hist, of P. E. I.] Many other papers were published in later years; the most prominent being the *Islander*, which appeared in 1842, and continued in existence for forty-two years. This paper along with the *Examiner*, edited by the Hon. Edward Whelan, a man of brilliant parts, now dead, had much influence over political affairs in the little colony.

The history of the newspaper press of British Columbia does not go beyond twenty-two years. The first attempt at journalistic enterprise was the Victoria *Gazette*, a daily published in 1858, by two Americans, who, however, stopped the issue in the following year. The next paper was the *Courrier de la Nouvelle Caledonie* printed by one Thornton, an Anglo-Frenchman, who had travelled all over the world. The somewhat notorious Marriott, of the San Francisco *News-Letter*, also, in 1859, published the Vancouver Island *Gazette*, but only for a while. It is a noteworthy fact, that the Cariboo *Sentinel*—now no longer in existence—was printed on a press sent out to Mgr. Demers, by the Roman Catholics of Paris. Even the little settlement of Emory has had its newspaper, the *Inland Sentinel*. The best known newspaper in the Pacific Province has always been, since 1858, the *British Colonist*, owned and edited originally by Hon. Amor de Cosmos, for some time Premier, and now a well-known member of the House of Commons, who made his paper a power in the little colony by his enterprise and forcible expression of opinion. The *Standard* is also another paper of political influence, and is published daily, like the *Colonist*. Two papers are printed in New Westminster, and one in Nanaimo; the total number in the province being five.

In the previous paragraphs, I have contained myself to the mention of a few facts in the early history of journalism in each of the Provinces of Canada. Proceeding now to a more extended review, we find that a few papers exercised from the outset a very decided influence in political affairs, and it is to these I propose now to refer, especially, before coming down to later times of extended political rights and consequent expansion of newspaper enterprise. The oldest newspaper now in Canada is the Montreal *Gazette*, which was first published as far back as 1787, by one Mesplet, in the French language. It ceased publication for a time, but reappeared about 1794, with Lewis Roy as printer. On the death of the latter, the establishment was assumed by E. Edwards, at No. 135 St. Paul Street, then the fashionable thoroughfare of the town. It was only a little affair, about the size of a large foolscap sheet, printed in small type in the two languages, and containing eight broad columns. In 1805, the Quebec *Mercury* was founded by Thomas Gary, a Nova Scotian lawyer, as an organ of the British inhabitants, who, at that time, formed a small but comparatively wealthy and influential section of the community. Mr. Gary was a man of scholarly attainments and a writer of considerable force. The *Mercury* had hardly been a year in existence, when its editor experienced the difficulty of writing freely in those troublous times, as he had to apologize for a too bold censure of the action of the dominant party in the Legislature. But this *contretemps* did not prevent him continuing in that vein of sarcasm of which he was a master, and evoking, consequently, the ire of the leading Liberals of those days—Stuart, Vanfelson, Papineau, Viger, and others. One of the results of his excessive freedom of speech was an attempt to punish him for a breach of privilege; but he remained concealed in his own house, where, like the conspirators of old times, he had a secret recess made for such purposes, and where he continued hurling his philippics against his adversaries with all that power of invective which would be used by a conscientious though uncompromising old Tory of those days, when party excitement ran so high. The Quebec *Gazette* was at that time, as in its first years, hardly more than a mere resume of news. [Footnote: From 1783 to 1792, the paper scarcely published a political 'leader,' and so fearful were printers of offending men in power, that the Montreal *Gazette*, so late as 1790, would not even indicate the locality in which a famous political banquet was held, on the occasion of the formation of a Constitutional Club, the principal object of which was to spread political knowledge throughout the country. See Garneau II. 197 and 206.] Hon. John Neilson assumed its editorship in 1796, and continued more or less to influence its columns whilst he remained in the Lower Canada Legislature. In 1808, Mr. Neilson enlarged the size of his paper, and published it twice a week, in order to meet the growing demand for political intelligence. The *Gazette* was trammelled for years by the fact that it was semi-official, and the vehicle of public notifications, but when, subsequently, [Footnote: In 1823, an Official Gazette was published by Dr. Fisher, Queen's Printer. Canadian Magazine,' p. 470.] this difficulty no longer existed, the paper, either under his own or his son's management, was independent, and, on the whole, moderate in tone whenever it expressed opinions on leading public questions. Mr. Neilson, from 1818, when he became a member of the Legislature, exercised a marked influence on the political discussions of his time, and any review of his career as journalist and politician would be necessarily a review of the political history of half a century. A constant friend of the French Canadians, a firm defender of British connection, never a violent, uncompromising partisan, but a man of cool judgment, he was generally able to perform good service to his party and country. As a public writer he was concise and argumentative, and influential, through the belief that men had in his sincerity and honesty of purpose.

In 1806, there appeared in Quebec a new organ of public opinion, which has continued to the present day to exercise much influence on the politics of Lower Canada. This was the *Canadien*, which was established in the fall of that year, chiefly through the exertions of Pierre Bedard, who was for a long while the leader of the French party in the Legislature, and at the same time chief editor of the new journal, which at once assumed a strong position as the exponent of the principles with which its French Canadian conductors were so long identified. It waged a bitter war against its adversaries, and no doubt had an important share in shaping the opinions and educating the public mind of the majority in the province. If it too frequently appealed to national prejudices, and assumed an uncompromising attitude when counsels of conciliation and moderation would have been wiser, we must make allowance for the hot temper of those times, and the hostile antagonism of races and parties, which the leaders on both sides were too often ready to foment, The editor of the *Canadien* was also punished by imprisonment for months, and the issue of the paper was stopped for a while on the order of Chief Justice Sewell, in the exciting times of that most arbitrary of military governors, Sir James Craig. The action of the authorities in this matter is now admitted to have been tyrannical and unconstitutional, and it is certainly an illustration of human frailty that this same M. Bedard, who suffered not a little from the injustice of his political enemies, should have shown such weakness—or, shall we say, Christian forbearance—in accepting, not long afterwards, a judgeship from the same Government which he had always so violently opposed, and from which he had suffered so much.

Whilst the *Canadien*, *Gazette*, and *Mercury* were, in Lower Canada, ably advocating their respective views on the questions of the day, the Press of Upper Canada was also exhibiting evidences of new vigour. The *Observer* was established at York, in 1820, and the *Canadian freeman* in 1825, the latter, an Opposition paper, well printed, and edited by Francis Collins who had also suffered at the hands of the ruling powers. An anecdote is related of the commencement of the journalistic career of this newspaper man of old times, which is somewhat characteristic of the feelings which animated the ruling powers of the day with respect to the mass of people who were not within the sacred pale. When Dr. Home gave up the publication of the *Gazette*, in whose office Collins had been for some time a compositor, the latter applied for the position, and was informed that 'the office would be given to none but a *gentleman*.'

This little incident recalls the quiet satire which Goldsmith levels in 'The Good-natured Man,' against just such absurd sensitiveness as

Collins had to submit to: —

FIRST FELLOW — The Squire has got spunk in him.

SECOND FELLOW — I loves to hear him sing, bekeays he never gives us nothing that's low.

THIRD FELLOW — O, damn anything that's low; I cannot bear it.

FOURTH FELLOW — The genteel thing is the genteel thing any time, if so be that a gentleman bees in a concatenation accordingly.

THIRD FELLOW — I likes the maxum of it. Master Muggins. What, though I am obligated to dance a bear, a man may be a gentleman for all that. May this be my poison, if my bear ever dances but to the very genteelest of tunes — 'Water Parted,' or 'The Minuet in Ariadne.'

No doubt this little episode made the disappointed applicant inveterate against the Government, for he commenced, soon afterwards, the publication of an Opposition paper, in which be exhibited the rude ability of an unpolished and half-educated man. [Footnote: C. Lindsey's 'Life of W. Lyon Mackenzie,' Vol. I., p. 112, note.]

Mr. W. Lyon Mackenzie appeared as a journalist for the first time in 1824, at Queenston, where he published the Colonial *Advocate*, on the model of Cobbett's *Register*, containing 32 pages, a form afterwards changed to the broad sheet. From the first it illustrated the original and eccentric talent of its independent founder. Italics and capitals, index hands and other typographic symbols, were scattered about with remarkable profusion, to give additional force and notoriety to the editorial remarks which were found on every page, according as the whim and inspiration of the editor dictated. The establishment of the paper was undoubtedly a bold attempt at a time when the province was but sparsely settled, and the circulation necessarily limited by the rarity of post-offices even in the more thickly-populated districts, and by the exorbitant rates of postage which amounted to eight hundred dollars a-year on a thousand copies. More than that, any independent expression of opinion was sure to evoke the ire of the orthodox in politics and religion, which in those days were somewhat closely connected. The *Advocate* was soon removed to York, and became from that time a political power, which ever and anon excited the wrath of the leaders of the opposite party, who induced some of their followers at last to throw the press and type of the obnoxious journal into the Bay, while they themselves, following the famous Wilkes' precedent, expelled Mackenzie from the legislature, and in defiance of constitutional law, declared him time and again ineligible to sit in the Assembly. The despotic acts of the reigning party, however, had the effect of awakening the masses to the necessity of supporting Mr. Mackenzie, and made him eventually a prominent figure in the politics of those disturbed times. The *Advocate* changed its name, a short time previous to 1837, to the *Constitution*, and then disappeared in the troublous days that ended with the flight of its indiscreet though honest editor. Contemporaneous with the *Advocate* were the *Loyalist*, the *Courier*, and the *Patriot*—the latter having first appeared at York in 1833. These three journals were Conservative, or rather Tory organs, and were controlled by Mr. Fothergill, Mr. Gurnett, and Mr. Dalton. Mr. Gurnett was for years after the Union the Police Magistrate of Toronto, while his old antagonist was a member of the Legislature, and the editor of the *Message*, a curiosity in political literature. Mr. Thomas Dalton was a very zealous advocate of British connection, and was one of the first Colonial writers to urge a Confederation of the Provinces; and if his zeal frequently carried him into the intemperate discussion of public questions the ardour of the times must be for him, as for his able, unselfish opponent, Mr. Mackenzie, the best apology.

Mrs. Jameson, who was by no means inclined to view Canadian affairs with a favourable eye, informs us that in 1836 there were some forty papers published in Upper Canada; of these, three were religious, namely, the *Christian Guardian*, the *Wesleyan Advocate*, and the *Church*. A paper in the German language was published at Berlin, in the Gore Settlement, for the use of the German settlers. Lower Canadian and American newspapers were also circulated in great numbers. She deprecates the abusive, narrow tone of the local papers, but at the same time admits—a valuable admission from one far from prepossessed in favour of Canadians—that, on the whole, the press did good in the absence and scarcity of books. In some of the provincial papers she 'had seen articles written with considerable talent;' among other things, 'a series of letters, signed Evans, on the subject of an education fitted for an agricultural people, and written with infinite good sense and kindly feeling.' At this time the number of newspapers circulated through the post-office in Upper Canada, and paying postage, was: Provincial papers, 178,065; United States and other foreign papers, 149,502. Adding 100,000 papers stamped, or free, there were some 427,567 papers circulated yearly among a population of 370,000, 'of whom perhaps one in fifty could read.' The narrow-mindedness of the country journals generally would probably strike an English *litterateur* like Mrs. Jameson with much force; little else was to be expected in a country, situated as Canada was then, with a small population, no generally diffused education, and imperfect facilities of communication with the great world beyond. In this comparatively isolated position, journalists might too often mistake

'The rustic murmur of their burgh
For the great wave that echoes round the world.'

Yet despite its defects, the journalism of Upper Canada was confessedly doing an important work in those backward days of Canadian development. The intelligence of the country would have been at a much lower ebb, without the dissemination of the press throughout the rural districts.

Whilst the journalists already named were contending in Upper Canada with fierce zeal for their respective parties, new names had appeared in the press of the other provinces. The *Canadien* was edited for years by M. Etienne Parent, except during its temporary suspension, from 1825 to 1831. His bold expression of opinion on the questions that forced a small party of his countrymen into an ill-advised rebellion sent him at last to prison; but, like others of his contemporaries, he eventually in more peaceful times received a recompense for his services by appointments in the public service, and died at last of a ripe old age a few months after his retirement from the Assistant-Secretaryship of State for the Dominion. In his hands the *Canadien* continued to wield great power among his compatriots, who have never failed to respect him as one of the ablest journalists their country has produced. His writings have not a little historical value, having been, in all cases where his feelings were not too deeply involved, characterized by breadth of view and critical acumen.

Whilst Gary, Neilson, Mackenzie, Parent, Dalton and Gurnett were the prominent journalists of the larger provinces, where politics were always at a fever heat, a young journalist first appeared in the Maritime Colonies, who was thenceforth to be a very prominent figure in the political contests of his native province. In 1827, Joseph Howe, whose family came of that sturdy, intelligent New England stock which has produced many men and women of great intellectual vigour, and who had been from an early age, like Franklin, brought up within the precincts of a printing office, bought out the *Weekly Chronicle*, of Halifax, and, changing its name to the *Acadian*, commenced his career as a public writer. Referring to the file of the *Acadian*, we see little to indicate unusual talent. It contains some lively sketches of natural scenery, some indifferent poetry, and a few common-place editorial contributions. A few months later he severed his connection with the *Acadian* and purchased the *Nova Scotian* from Mr. G. R. Young, the brother of the present Chief-Justice, a man of large knowledge and fine intellect. It was a courageous undertaking for so young a man, as he was only 24 years of age when he assumed the control of so prominent a paper; but the rulers of the dominant official party soon found in him a vigorous opponent and a zealous advocate of Liberal opinions. It is a noteworthy fact that Mr. Howe, like Mr. Mackenzie in Upper Canada, made himself famous at the outset of his career by pleading on his own behalf in a case of libel. Mr. Mackenzie had been prosecuted for an alleged libel circulated during a political contest with Mr. Small, and defended his own cause so successfully that the jury gave him a verdict; and they are even said, according to Mr. Lindsey's 'Life of Mr. Mackenzie,' to have debated among themselves whether it was not competent for them to award damages to the defendant for the annoyance of a frivolous prosecution. Mr. Howe's debut as an advocate was in connection with a matter of much graver importance. He had the courage, at a time when there existed many abuses apparently without hope of redress, to attack the Halifax Bench of Magistrates, little autocrats in their way, a sort of Venetian Council, and the consequence was a criminal indictment for libel. He determined to get up his own case, and, after several days' close study of authorities, he went to the jury in the Old Court Room, now turned into the Legislative Library, and succeeded in obtaining a glorious acquittal and no small amount of popular applause for his moral courage on this memorable occasion. The subsequent history of his career justified the confidence which his friends thenceforth reposed in him. His indefatigable industry, added to his great love of the masters of English literature, soon gave vigour and grace to his style, whilst his natural independence of spirit that could little brook control in any shape, and his innate hatred of political despotism, soon led him to attack boldly the political abuses of the day. The history of Joseph Howe from that day was a history of the triumph of Liberal principles and of responsible government in Nova Scotia. As a versatile writer, he has had no superior in Canada, for he brought to the political controversies of his time the aid of powerful invective and cutting satire; whilst, on occasions when party strife was hushed, he could exhibit all the evidences of his cultivated intellect and sprightly humour.

The new era of Canadian journalism commenced with the settlement of the political difficulties which so long disturbed the provinces, and with the concession of responsible government, which gave a wider range to the intellect of public writers. The leading papers, in 1840, were the Montreal *Gazette*, the Montreal *Herald*, the *Canadien*, the Quebec *Gazette*, the Quebec *Mercury*, in Lower Canada; the *British Colonist*, *British Whig*, and *Examiner*, in Upper Canada; the *Nova Scotian* and *Acadian Recorder*, in Nova Scotia; the *News*, in New Brunswick. The *Colonist* was founded at Toronto, in 1838, by Hugh Scobie, under the name of the *Scotsman* — changed to the former title in the third number — and from the outset took a high position as an independent organ of the Conservative party. The copy of the first number, before me, is quite an improvement on the *Gazette* and *Mercury* of Quebec, as published in the early part of the century. It contains some twenty-four columns, on a sheet about as large as the Ottawa *Free Press*. It contains several short editorials, a resume of news, and terse legislative reports. Among the advertisements is one of the New York *Albion*, which, for so many years, afforded an intellectual treat to the people of all the provinces; for it was in its columns they were able to read the best productions of Marryatt and other English authors, not easily procurable in those early times; besides being annually presented with engravings of merit—a decided improvement on the modern chromo—from the paintings of eminent artists; engravings which are still to be seen in thousands of Canadian homes, and which, in their way, helped to cultivate taste among the masses, by whom good pictures of that class could not be easily procured.

The Examiner was started at Toronto, on the appointment of Lord Durham to the Government of Canada, as an organ of the Liberal party, by Mr. Francis Hincks, a young Irishman, who, from his first arrival in Canada, attracted attention as a financier and a journalist. *The Examiner*, however, had not a long existence, for Sir Francis Hincks—we give him his later title, won after years of useful public service as journalist and statesman—proceeded, in 1843, to Montreal, where he established the *Pilot*, which had much influence as an organ of the party led by Baldwin and Lafontaine. In 1844, a young Scotchman, Mr. George Brown, began to be a power in the politics of the Canadian Provinces. He was first connected with *The Banner*, founded in the interest of the Free Church party; but the Liberals found it necessary to have a special organ, and the result was the establishment, in 1844, of the Toronto *Globe*, at first a weekly, then a tri-weekly, and eventually the most widely circulated and influential daily paper in British North America. During the thirty-five years Mr. Brown remained connected with that journal it invariably bore the impress of his powerful intellect. The *Globe* and George Brown were always synonymous in the public mind, and the influence he exercised over his party—no doubt a tyrannical influence at times—proved the power that a man of indomitable will and tenacity of purpose can exercise in the control of a political organ. From 1844 to the present time the newspaper press made progress equal to the growth of the provinces in population, wealth and intelligence. The rapid improvement in the internal communications of the country, the increase of post offices and the cheapness of postage, together with the remarkable development of public education, especially in Upper Canada, naturally gave a great impulse to newspaper enterprise in all the large cities and towns. *Le Journal de Quebec* was established in 1842 by the Hon Joseph Cauchon, from that time a force in political life. Another journal, the *Minerve*, of Montreal, which had been founded in 1827 by M. Morin, but had ceased publication during the troubles of 1837-8, re-appeared again in 1842, and assumed that influential position as an exponent of the Bleus which it has continued to occupy to the present. *Le Pays*, *La Patrie*, and *L'Avenir* were other Canadian papers, supporting the Rouges—the latter having been established in 1848, and edited by *l'enfant terrible*, M. J. B. Eric Dorion, a brother of Sir Antoine Dorion. In Upper Canada, Mr. R. Reid Smiley established, during 1846, the Hamilton *Spectator*, as a tri-weekly, which was changed to a daily issue in 1852. In 1848, Mr. W. Macdougall appeared for the first time as a journalist, in connection with the *Canada Farmer*; but when that journal was merged into the *Canada Agriculturist*, he founded the *North American*, which exerted no small influence as a trenchant, vigorous exponent of Reform principles, until it was amalgamated, in 1857, with the *Globe*. In 1852 the *Leader* was established, at Toronto, by Mr. James Beaty—the old *Patriot* becoming its weekly issue—and during the years it remained under the editorial management of Mr. Charles Lindsey—a careful, graceful writer of large knowledge —it exercised much influence as an exponent of the views of the Liberal Conservative party; but soon after his retirement it lost its position, and died at last from pure inanition and incapacity to keep up with the progressive demands of modern journalism. In 1857, Mr. McGee made his appearance in Canada as the editor of the Montreal *New Era*, in which he illustrated for some years the brilliancy of his style and his varied attainments. The history of journalism, indeed, from 1840 to 1867, brings before us a number of able writers, whose names are remembered with pride by all who were connected with them and had opportunities, not merely of reading their literary contributions, but of personally associating with men of such varied accomplishments and knowledge of the Canadian world. Morrison, Sheppard, Penny, Chamberlin, Brown, Lindsey, Macdougall, Hogan, McGee, Whelan, P. S. Hamilton, T. White, Derome, Cauchon, Jos. Doutre, were the most distinguished writers of an epoch which was famous for its political and industrial progress. But of all that brilliant phalanx, Mr. White alone contributes, with more or less regularity, to the press, whilst all the others are either dead or engaged in other occupations. [Footnote: Mr. McGee was assassinated in 1868. The circumstances of the death of John Sheridan Hogan, in 1859, were not known till years afterwards, when one of the infamous Don Gang revealed the story of his wretched end. Then we have the great journalist and leader of the Liberal party in Upper Canada also dying from the effects of a pistol-wound at the hands of a drunken reprobate. Hon. Edward Whelan, of Charlottetown, died years ago. Mr. Morrison died whilst editor of the Toronto *Daily Telegraph*. Mr. Sheppard was, when last heard of, in New York, in connection with the press. Mr. Lindsey is Registrar of Toronto. Hon. Joseph Cauchon is Lieutenant-Governor of Manitoba. Mr. Chamberlin is Queen's Printer at Ottawa, and his partner on the *Gazette*, Mr. Lowe, is also in the Civil service. Mr. Derome died only a few weeks ago. Mr. Penny is a Senator. Mr. McDongall is a member of the Commons, and lives in Ottawa. Mr. Doutre is at the head of his profession in Quebec. Mr. Belford, of the *Mail*, died a few weeks ago at Ottawa. Besides those older journalists mentioned in the text, younger men, like Mr. Descelles and Mr. Dansereau, of the *Minerve*, and Mr. Patteson, of the *Mail*, have also received positions recently in the public service. Mr. Edward McDonald, who founded, with Mr. Garvie, the Halifax *Citizen*, in opposition to the *Reporter*, of which the present writer was editor, died Collector of the Port. Mr. Bowell, of the Belleville *Intelligencer*, is now Minister of Customs. The list might be extended indefinitely.]

Since 1867, the *Mail*, established in 1873 as the chief organ of the Liberal Conservatives, has come to the front rank in journalism, and is a powerful rival of the *Globe*, while the *Colonist*, *Leader*, and other papers which once played an important part in the political drama, are forgotten, like most political instruments that have done their service and are no longer available. Several of the old journals so long associated with the history of political and intellectual activity in this country, however, still exist as influential organs. The Quebec *Gazette* was, some years ago, merged into another Quebec paper—having become long before a memorial of the past in its appearance and dullness, a sort of Rip Van Winkle in the newspaper world. The *Canadien* has always had its troubles; but, nevertheless, it continues to have influence in the Quebec district, and the same may be said of the *Journal de Quebec*, though the writer who first gave it power in politics is now keeping petty state in the infant Province of the West. The Quebec *Mercury* still exists, though on a very small scale of late. The Montreal *Gazette* (now the oldest paper in Canada), the Montreal *Herald*, the *Minerve*, the Hamilton *Spectator*, and the Brockville *Recorder* (established in 1820), are still exercising political influence as of old. The St. John *News* and the Halifax *Acadian Recorder* are still vigorously carried on. The Halifax *Chronicle* remains the leading Liberal organ in Nova Scotia, though the journalist whose name was so long associated with it in the early days of its influence died a few years ago in the old Government House, within whose sacred walls he was not permitted to enter in the days of his fierce controversy with Lord Falkland. In its later days, the Hon. William Annand, lately in the employment of the Dominion Government in London, was nominally the Editor-in-Chief, but the Hon. Jonathan McCully, Hiram Blanchard, and William Garvie were among those who contributed largely to its editorial columns—able political writers not long since dead. The public journals of this country are now so numerous that it would take several pages to enumerate them; hardly a village of importance throughout Canada but has one or more weeklies. In 1840 there were, as accurately as I have been able to ascertain, only 65 papers in all Canada, including the Maritime Provinces. In 1857, there were 243 in all; in 1862 some 320, and in 1870 the number had increased to 432, of which Ontario alone owned 255. The number has not much increased since then—the probable number being now 465, of which 56, at least, appear daily. [Footnote: The data for 1840 are taken from Martin's 'Colonial Empire,' and Mrs. Jameson's account. The figures for 1857 are taken from Lovell's 'Canada Directory;' the figures for 1880 from the lists in Commons and Senate Reading Rooms. The last census returns for the four old Provinces give only 308 printing establishments, employing 3,400 hands, paying $1,200,000 in wages, and producing articles to the worth of $3,420,202. Although not so stated, these figures probably include job as well as newspaper offices—both being generally combined—and newspapers where no job work is done are obviously left out.] The Post Office statistics show in 1879, that 4,085,454 lbs. of newspapers, at one cent per lb. passed through the post offices of the Dominion, and 5,610,000 copies were posted otherwise. Nearly three millions and a half of papers were delivered under the free delivery system in the cities of Halifax, Hamilton, London, Montreal, Quebec, Ottawa, St. John, and Toronto. Another estimate gives some 30,000,000 of papers passing through the Post Office in the course of a year, of which probably two thirds, or 20,000,000, are Canadian. These figures do not, however, represent any thing like the actual circulation of the Canadian papers, as the larger proportion are immediately delivered to subscribers by carriers in the cities and towns. The census of 1870 in the United States showed the total annual circulation of the 5,871 newspapers in that country to be, 1,508,548,250, or an average of forty for each person in the Republic, or one for every inhabitant in the world. Taking the same basis for our calculation, we may estimate there are upwards of 160,000,000 copies of newspapers annually distributed to our probable population of four millions of people. The influence which the newspaper press must exercise upon the intelligence of the masses is consequently obvious.

The names of the journals that take the front rank, from the enterprise and ability with which they are conducted, will occur to every one *au courant* with public affairs: the *Globe* and *Mail*, in Toronto; the *Gazette* and *Herald*, in Montreal; the *Chronicle* (in its 34th year) and *Mercury*, in Quebec; the *Spectator* and *Times*, in Hamilton; the *Free Press* and *Advertiser*, in London; the *British Whig* (in its 46th year) and *Daily News*, in Kingston; *Citizen* and *Free Press*, in Ottawa; *News*, *Globe*, *Telegraph*, and *Sun*, in St. John, N. B.; *Herald* and *Chronicle*, in Halifax; the *Examiner* and *Patriot*, in Prince Edward Island, are the chief exponents of the principles of the Conservative and Liberal party. Besides these political organs the Montreal *Star* and *Witness*, and the Toronto *Telegram* have a large circulation, and are more or less independent in their opinions. Among the French papers, besides those referred to above, we have the *Courrier de Montreal* (1877), *Nouveau Monde* (1867), *L'Evenement* (1867), *Courrier d'Ottawa*, now *le Canada* (1879), *Franco Canadien* (1857), which enjoy more or less influence in the Province of Quebec. Perhaps no fact illustrates more strikingly the material and mental activity of the Dominion than the number of newspapers now published in the new Province of the North-West. The first paper in that region appeared in 1859, when Messrs. Buckingham & Coldwell conveyed to Fort Garry their

press and materials in an ox cart, and established the little *Nor'
Wester* immediately under the walls of the fort. Now there are three
dailies published in the City of Winnipeg alone—all of them well
printed and fairly edited—and at least sixteen papers in all appear
periodically through the North-West. The country press—that is to
say, the press published outside the great centres of industrial and
political activity—has remarkably improved in vigour within a few
years; and the metropolitan papers are constantly receiving from its
ranks new and valuable accessions, whilst there remain connected
with it, steadily labouring with enthusiasm in many cases, though
the pecuniary rewards are small, an indefatigable band of terse,
well-informed writers, who exercise no mean influence within the
respective spheres of their operations. The Sarnia *Observer*, Sher-
brooke *Gazette*, Stratford *Beacon*, Perth *Courier* (1834), Lindsay *Post*,
Guelph *Mercury* (1845), Yarmouth *Herald*, Peterboro *Review*, St.
Thomas *Journal*, *News of St. Johns* (Q), *Courrier de St. Hyacinthe*, Car-
leton *Sentinel*, Maritime *Farmer*, are among the many journals which
display no little vigour in their editorials and skill in the selection of
news and literary matter. During the thirteen years that have
elapsed since Confederation new names have been inscribed on the
long roll of Canadian journalists. Mr. Gordon Brown still remains in
the editorial chair of the *Globe*, one of the few examples we find in
the history of Canadian journalism of men who have not been carried away by the excitement of politics or the attraction of a soft
place in the public service. The names of White, McCulloch, Farrar,
Rattray, G. Stewart, jr., M. J. Griffin, Carroll Ryan, Stewart (Montreal *Herald*), Stewart (Halifax *Herald*), Sumichrast, Fielding, Elder,
Geo. Johnson, Blackburn (London *Free Press*), Cameron (London
Advertiser), Davin, Dymond, Pirie, D. K. Brown, Mackintosh, Mac-
ready, Livingstone, Ellis, Houde, Vallee, Desjardins, Tarte, Faucher
de St. Maurice, Fabre, Tasse, L'O. David, are among the prominent
writers on the most widely circulated English and French Canadian
papers.

In the necessarily limited review I have been forced to give of the
progress of journalism in Canada, I have made no mention of the
religious press which has been established, in the large cities princi-
pally, as the exponent of the views of particular sects. The Methodist body has been particularly successful in this line of business, in

comparison with other denominations. The *Christian Guardian*, established at Toronto in 1829, under the editorial supervision of Rev. Egerton Ryerson, continues to exhibit its pristine vigour under the editorship of the Rev. Mr. Dewart. The organ of the same body in the Maritime Provinces is the *Wesleyan*, edited by Rev. T. Watson Smith, and is fully equal in appearance and ability to its Western contemporary. The Baptists, Presbyterians, Episcopal Methodists and Congregationalists, have also exponents of their particular views. The Church of England has made many attempts to establish denominational organs on a successful basis, but very few of them have ever come up to the expectations of their promoters in point of circulation—the old *Church* having been, on the whole, the most ably conducted. At present there are three papers in the west, representing different sections of the Church. The Roman Catholics have also their organs, not so much religious as political—the St. John *Freeman*, edited by the Hon. Mr. Anglin, is the most remarkable for the ability and vigour with which it has been conducted as a supporter of the views of the Liberal party in the Dominion, as well as of the interests of the Roman Catholic body. In all there are some thirty papers published in the Dominion, professing to have the interests of certain sects particularly at heart. [Footnote: It is noteworthy that the Canadian religions press has never attained the popularity of the American Denominational Journals, which are said to have an aggregate circulation of nearly half of the secular press.]

The *Canadian Illustrated News* and *L'Opinion Publique*, which owe their establishment to the enterprise of Mr. Desbarats, a gentleman of culture, formerly at the head of the old Government Printing Office, are among the examples of the new vigour and ability that have characterized Canadian journalistic enterprise of recent years. The illustrations in the *News* are, on the whole well executed, and were it possible to print them on the superior tinted paper of the *Graphic*, and it would be possible if the people were willing to pay the expense, they would compare more favourably than they do with the impressions of the older papers published in New York and London. In its prints of native scenery, and portraits of deceased Canadians of merit, the *News* is a valuable and interesting addition to journalism in this country, and will be found most useful to the future generations who will people the Dominion. Nor does Canada now lack an imitator of *Punch*, in the humorous line. It is noteworthy that whilst America has produced humorists like 'Sam Slick,' Artemus Ward, Mark Twain, and others, no American rival to *Punch* has yet appeared in Boston or New York. The attempts that have heretofore been made have been generally coarse caricatures—for example, the political cartoons in *Harper's Weekly*, which are never characterized by those keen artistic touches that make *Punch* so famous. Previous efforts in this field of political and social satire in Canada have always failed for want of support, as well as from the absence of legitimate humour. The oldest satirical sheet was *Le Fantastique*, published at Quebec by N. Aubin, who was a very bitter partisan, and was sent to gaol in 1838 for the expression of his opinions. The *Grumbler* was a more creditable effort made in Toronto some quarter of a century ago, to illustrate and hit off the political and social foibles of the day in Canada. But it has been left for Mr. Bengough in these times to rise in *Grip* far above all previous attempts in the same direction, and 'to show up' very successfully, and generally with much humour, certain salient features of our contemporary history.

The influence of the press, during the century, must be measured by the political intelligence and activity of the people. Only in the United States are the masses as well informed on the public questions of the day as are the majority of Canadians, and this fact must be attributed, in a large measure, to the efforts of journalists to educate the people and stimulate their mental faculties. When education was at a low ebb indeed, when the leading and wealthier class was by no means too anxious to increase the knowledge of the people, the press was the best vehicle of public instruction. No doubt it often abused its trust, and forgot the responsibilities devolving on it; no doubt its conductors were too frequently animated by purely selfish motives, yet, taking the good with the evil, the former was predominant as a rule. It is only necessary to consider the number of journalists who have played an important part in Parliament, to estimate the influence journalism must have exerted on the political fortunes of Canada. The names of Neilson, Bedard, W. L. Mackenzie, Hincks, Howe, Brown, and Macdougall, will recall remarkable epochs in our history. But it is not only as a political engine that the press has had a decided beneficial effect upon the public intelligence; it has generally been alive to the social and moral questions of the hour, and exposed religions charlatanry, and arrested the progress of dangerous social innovations, with the same fearlessness and vigour which it has shown in the case of political abuses. Political controversy, no doubt, has too often degenerated into licentiousness, and public men have been too often maligned, simply because they were political opponents—an evil which weakens the influence of journalism to an incalculable degree, because the people begin at last to attach little or no importance to charges levelled recklessly against public men. But it is not too much to say that the press of all parties is commencing to recognise its responsibilities to a degree that would not have been possible a few years ago. It is true the ineffable meanness of old times of partisan controversy will crop out constantly in certain quarters, and political writers are not always the safest guides in times of party excitement. But there is a healthier tone in public discussion, and the people are better able to eliminate the truth and come to a correct conclusion. Personalities are being gradually discouraged, and appeals more frequently made to the reason rather than to the passion and prejudice of party—a fact in itself some evidence of the progress of the readers in culture. The great change in the business basis on which the leading newspapers are now-a-days conducted, of itself must tend to modify political acrimony, and make them safer public guides. A great newspaper now-a-days must be conducted on the same principles on which any other business is carried on. The expenses of a daily journal are now so great that it requires the outlay of large capital to keep it up to the requirements of the time; in fact, it can best be done by joint-stock companies, rather than by individual effort. Slavish dependence on a Government or party, as in the old times of journalism, can never make a newspaper successful as a financial speculation, nor give it that circulation on which its influence in a large measure depends. The journal of the present day is a compilation of telegraphic despatches from all parts of the world, and of reports of all matters of local and provincial importance, with one or more columns of concise editorial comment on public topics of general interest: and the success with which this is done is the measure of its circulation and influence. Both the *Globe* and *Mail* illustrate this fact very forcibly; both journals being good *newspapers*, in every sense of the term, read by Conservatives and Liberals, irrespective of political opinions, although naturally depending for their chief support on a particular party. In no better way can we illustrate the great change that has taken place within less than half a century in the newspaper enterprise of this country than by comparing a copy of a journal of 1839 with one of 1880. Taking, in the first place, the issue of the Toronto *British Colonist,* for the 23rd October, 1839, we have before us a sheet, as previously stated, of twenty-four columns, twelve of which are advertisements and eight of extracts, chiefly from New York papers. Not a single editorial appeared in this number, though prominence was given to a communication describing certain riotous proceedings, in which prominent 'blues' took part, on the occasion of a public meeting attempted to be held at a Mr. Davis's house on Yonge Street, for the purpose of considering important changes about to take place in the political Constitution of the Canadas. Mr. Poulett Thompson had arrived in the St. Lawrence on the 16th, but the *Colonist* was only able to announce the fact on the 23rd of the month. New York papers took four days to reach Toronto—a decided improvement, however, on old times—and these afforded Canadian editors the most convenient means of culling foreign news. Only five lawyers advertised their places of business; Mr. and Mrs. Crombie announced the opening of their well-known schools. McGill College, at last, advertised that it was open to students—an important event in the educational history of Canada, which, however, received no editorial comment in the paper. We come upon a brief advertisement from Messrs. Armour & Ramsay, the well-known booksellers; but the only book they announced was that work so familiar to old-time students, 'Walkinghame's Arithmetic.' Another literary announcement was the publication of a work, by the Rev. R. Murray, of Oakville, on the 'Tendency and Errors of Temperance Societies'—then in the infancy of their progress in Upper Canada. One of the most encouraging notices was that of the Montreal Type Foundry, which was beginning to compete with American establishments, also advertised in the same issue—an evidence of the rapid progress of printing in Canada. Only one steamer was advertised, the *Gore,* which ran between Toronto and Hamilton; she was described as 'new, splendid, fast-sailing, and elegantly fitted up,' and no doubt she was, compared with the old batteaux and schooners which, not long before, had kept up communication with other parts of the Province. On the whole, this issue illustrated the fact that Toronto was making steady progress, and Upper Canada was no longer a mere wilderness. Many of my readers will recall those days, for I am writing of times within the memory of many Upper Canadians.

Now take an ordinary issue of the *Mail*, printed on the same day, in the same city, only forty-one years later. We see a handsome paper of eight closely-printed pages — each larger than a page of the *Colonist* — and fifty-six columns, sixteen of which are devoted to advertisements illustrative of the commercial growth, not only of Toronto, but of Ontario at large — advertisements of Banking, Insurance and Loan Companies, representing many millions of capital; of Railway and Steamship Lines, connecting Toronto daily with all parts of America and Europe; of various classes of manufactures, which have grown up in a quarter of a century or so. No less than five notices of theatrical and other amusements appear; these entertainments take place in spacious, elegant halls and opera houses, instead of the little, confined rooms which satisfied the citizens of Toronto only a few years ago. Some forty barristers and attorneys, physicians and surgeons — no, not all gentlemen, but one a lady — advertise their respective offices, and yet these are only representative of the large number of persons practising these professions in the same city. Leaving the advertisements and reviewing the reading matter, we find eleven columns devoted to telegraphic intelligence from all parts of the world where any event of interest has occurred a day or two before. Several columns are given up to religious news, including a lengthy report of the proceedings of the Baptist Union, meeting, for the first time, under an Act of Parliament of 1880 — an Association intended for the promotion of missions, *literature*, and church work, into which famous John Bunyan would have heartily thrown himself, no longer in fear of being cast into prison. Four columns are taken up with sports and pastimes, such as lacrosse, the rifle, rowing, cricket, curling, foot-ball, hunting — illustrative of the growing taste among all classes of young men for such healthy recreation. Perhaps no feature of the paper gives more conclusive evidence of the growth of the city and province than the seven columns specially set apart to finance, commerce and marine intelligence, and giving the latest and fullest intelligence of prices in all places with which Canada has commercial transactions. Nearly one column of the smallest type is necessary to announce the arrivals and departures of the steam-tugs, propellers, schooners and other craft which make up the large inland fleet of the Western Province. We find reports of proceedings in the Courts in Toronto and elsewhere, besides many items of local interest. Five columns are made up of editorials and editorial briefs, the latter an interesting feature of modern journalism. The 'leader' is a column in length, and is a sarcastic commentary on the 'fallacious hopes' of the Opposition; the next article is an answer to one in the London *Economist*, devoted to the vexed question of protective duties in the Colonies; another refers to modern 'literary criticism,' one of the strangest literary products of this busy age of intellectual development. In all we have thirty-six columns of reading matter, remarkable for literary execution and careful editing, as well as for the moderate tone of its political criticism. It will be seen that there is only one advertisement of books in the columns of this issue, but the reason is that it is the custom only to advertise new works on Saturday, when the paper generally contains twelve pages, or eighty-four columns. On the whole, the issue of a very prominent Canadian paper illustrates not only the material development of Ontario in its commercial and advertising columns, but also the mental progress of the people, who demand so large an amount of reading matter at the cost of so much money and mental labour.

As the country increases in wealth and population, the Press must become undoubtedly still more a profession to which men of the highest ability and learning will attach themselves permanently, instead of being too often attracted, as heretofore, by the greater pecuniary rewards offered by other pursuits in life. Horace Greeley, Dana, Curtis, Whitelaw Reid and Bryant are among the many illustrious examples that the neighbouring States afford of men to whom journalism has been a profession, valued not simply for the temporary influence and popularity it gives, but as a great and powerful organ of public education on all the live questions of the day. The journals whose conductors are known to be above the allurements of political favour, even while they consistently sustain the general policy of a party, are those which most obviously become the true exponents of a sound public opinion, and the successful competitor for public favour in this, as in all other countries enjoying a popular system of government.

CHAPTER IV.

NATIVE LITERATURE.

Lord Durham wrote, over fifty [Errata: (from final page) for *fifty* read *forty*.] years ago, of the French Canadians: 'They are a people without a history and a literature.' He was very ignorant, assuredly, of the deep interest that attaches to the historic past of the first pioneers in Canada, and had he lived to the present day, he would have blotted out the first part of the statement. But he was right enough when he added that the French Canadians had, at that time, no literature of their own. During the two centuries and more that Canada remained a French Colony, books were neither read nor written; they were only to be seen in the educational establishments, or in a very few private houses, in the later days of the colony. [Footnote: The priests appear to have only encouraged books of devotion. La Hontan mentions an incident of a priest coming into his room and tearing up a book; but the library of that gay gentleman was hardly very select and proper.] An intellectual torpor was the prevailing feature of the French *regime*. Only now and then do we meet in the history of those early times with the name of a man residing in the colony with some reputation for his literary or scientific attainments. The genial, chatty L'Escarbot has left us a pleasant volume of the early days of Acadie, when De Monts and De Poutrincourt were struggling to establish Port Royal. The works of the Jesuits Lafitau and Charlevoix are well known to all students of the historic past of Canada. The Marquis de la Galissoniere was the only man of culture among the functionaries of the French dominion. Parkman tells us that the physician Sarrazin, whose name still clings to the pitcher-plant (*Sarracenia purpurea*) was for years the only real medical man in Canada, and was chiefly dependent for his support on the miserable pittance of three hundred francs yearly, given him by the king. Yet it would be a mistake to suppose there was no cultivated society in Canada. The navigator Bougainville tells us, that, though education was so defective, the Canadians were naturally very intelligent, and their accent was as good as that of the Parisians. Another well-informed writer says 'there was a select little society in Quebec, which wants nothing to make it agreeable. In the salons of the wives of the Governor and Intendant one finds circles as brilliant as in other countries. Science and the Fine Arts have their turn, and conversation does not flag. The Canadians breathe from their birth an air of liberty, which makes them very pleasant in the intercourse of life, and our language is nowhere more purely spoken.' But the people outside of the little coterie, of which this writer speaks so flatteringly, had no opportunities whatever of following the progress of new ideas in the parent state. What learning there was could only be found among the priests, to whom we owe 'Les Relations des Jesuites,' among other less notable productions. The Roman Catholic Church, being everywhere a democracy, the humblest *habitant* might enter its ranks and aspire to its highest dignities. Consequently we find the pioneers of that Church, at the very outset, affording the Canadian an opportunity, irrespective of birth or wealth, of entering within its pale. But apart from this class, there was no inducement offered to Canadian intellect in those times.

The Conquest robbed the country of a large proportion of the best class of the Canadian *noblesse*, and many years elapsed before the people awoke from their mental slumber. The press alone illustrated the literary capacity of the best intellects for very many years after the fall of Quebec. We have already read how many political writers of eminence were born with the endowment of the Canadian with political rights, which aroused him from his torpor and gave his mental faculties a new impulse. The only works, however, of national importance which issued from the press, from the Conquest to the Union of 1840, were Mr. Joseph Bouchette's topographical descriptions of British North America, which had to be published in England at a great expense; but these books, creditable as they were to the ability and industry of the author, and useful as they certainly were to the whole country, could never enter into general circulation. They must always remain, however, the most creditable specimens of works of that class ever published in any country. The first volume of poetry, written by a French Canadian, was published in 1830, by M. Michel Bibaud, who was also the editor of the 'Bibliotheque Canadienne,' and 'Le Magazin du Bas Canada,' periodicals very short lived, though somewhat promising.

From the year 1840, commenced a new era in French Canadian letters, as we can see by reference to the pages of several periodical publications, which were issued subsequently. 'Le Repertoire National,' published from 1848 to 1850, contained the first efforts of those writers who could fairly lay claim to be the pioneers of French Canadian Literature. This useful publication was followed by the 'Soirees Canadiennes,' and 'Le Foyer Canadien,' which also gave a new impulse to native talent, and those who wish to study the productions of the early days of French Canadian literature will find much interest and profit in the pages of these characteristic publications, as well as in the 'Revue Canadienne,' of these later times. From the moment the intellect of the French Canadian was stimulated by a patriotic love for the past history and traditions of his country, volumes of prose and poetry of more or less merit commenced to flow regularly from the press. Two histories of undoubted value have been written by French Canadians, and these are the works of Garneau and Ferland. The former is the history of the French Canadian race, from its earliest days to the Union of 1840. It is written with much fervour, from the point of view of a French Canadian, imbued with a strong sense of patriotism, and is the best monument ever raised to Papineau; for that brilliant man is M. Garneau's hero, to whose political virtues he is always kind, and to whose political follies he is too often insensible. Old France, too, is to him something more than a memory; he would fix her history and traditions deep in the hearts of his countrymen; but great as is his love for her, he does not fail to show, even while pointing out the blunders of British Ministries, that Canada, after all, must be happier under the new, than under the old, *regime*. The 'Cours d'Histoire du Canada' was unfortunately never completed by the Abbe Ferland, who was Professor of the Faculty of Arts in the Laval University. Yet the portion that he was able to finish before his death displays much patient research and narrative skill, and justly entitles him to a first place among French Canadian historians.

In romance, several attempts have been made by French Canadians, but without any marked success, except in two instances. M. de

Gaspe, when in his seventieth year, described in simple, natural language, in 'Les Anciens Canadiens,' the old life of his compatriots. M. Gerin Lajoie attempted, in 'Jean Rivard,' to portray the trials and difficulties of the Canadian pioneer in the backwoods. M. Lajoie is a pleasing writer, and discharged his task with much fidelity to nature. It is somewhat noteworthy that the author, for many years assistant librarian of the library of Parliament, should have selected for his theme the struggles of a man of action in a new country; for no subject could apparently be more foreign to the tastes of the genial, scholarly man of letters, who, seemingly overcome by the torpor of official life in a small city, or the slight encouragement given to Canadian books, never brought to full fruition the intellectual powers which his early efforts so clearly showed him to possess.

In poetry, the French Canadian has won a more brilliant success than in the sister art of romance. Four names are best known in Quebec for the smoothness of the versification, the purity of style, and the poetic genius which some of their works illustrate. These are, MM. Le May, Cremazie, Sulte, and Frechette. M. Cremazie's elegy on 'Les Morts' is worthy of even Victor Hugo. M. Frechette was recognised long ago in Paris as a young man of undoubted promise 'on account of the genius which reflects on his fatherland a gleam of his own fame.' Since M. Frechette has been removed from the excitement of politics, he has gone back to his first mistress, and has won for himself and native province the high distinction of being crowned the poet of the year by the French Academy. M. Frechette has been fortunate in more than one respect,—in having an Academy to recognise his poetic talent, and again, in being a citizen of a nationality more ready than the English section of our population to acknowledge that literary success is a matter of national pride.

The French Canadians have devoted much time and attention to that fruitful field of research which the study of the customs and antiquities of their ancestors opens up to them. The names of Jacques Viger and Faribault, Sir Louis Lafontaine, the Abbes Laverdiere, and Verrault are well known as those of men who devoted themselves to the accumulation of valuable materials illustrative of the historic past, as the library of Laval University can testify. The

74

edition of Champlain's works, by the Abbe Laverdiere for some years librarian of Laval, is a most creditable example of critical acumen and typographical skill. In the same field there is much yet to be explored by the zealous antiquarian who has the patience to delve among the accumulations of matter that are hidden in Canadian and European archives. This is a work, however, which can be best done by the State; and it is satisfactory to know that something has been attempted of late years in this direction by the Canadian Government—the collection of the Haldimand papers, for instance. But we are still far behind our American neighbours in this respect, as their State libraries abundantly prove.

The Canadian ballad was only known for years by the favourite verses written by the poet Moore, which, however musical, have no real semblance to the veritable ballads with which the voyageurs have for centuries kept time as they pushed over the lakes and rivers of Canada and the North-west. Dr. Larue and M. Ernest Gagnon have given us a compilation of this interesting feature of French Canadian literature, which is hardly yet familiar to the English population of Canada.

Other French Canadian names occur to the writer, but it is impossible to do justice to them in this necessarily limited review. 'Les Legendes,' of the Abbe Casgrain, 'Les Pionniers de l'Ouest,' of M. Joseph Tasse, and the works of M. Faucher de St. Maurice, are among other illustrations of the national spirit that animates French Canadian writers, and makes them deservedly popular among their compatriots.

If we now turn to the literary progress of the English-speaking people of Canada, we see some evidences of intellectual activity from an early time in the history of these colonies. During the two decades immediately preceding the Union of 1840, there was a cultured society in all the larger centres of intelligence. In official circles there was always found much culture and refinement, and the inmates of "Government House," in the several capitals, then as now, dispensed a graceful hospitality and contributed largely to the pleasures of the little society of which they were the leaders by virtue of their elevated position. Social circles which could boast of the presence of Mr. John Galt, author of 'Laurie Todd,' and other works of note in their day, of Mr. and Mrs. Jameson, who lived some years in Toronto, of the Stricklands, of Judge Haliburton, of learned divines, astute lawyers and politicians, and clever journalists, could not have been altogether behind older communities. From one of the magazines, published in 1824, we learn that there were some libraries in the large towns of Quebec, Montreal, York, Kingston, and Halifax; that belonging to the Parliament at Quebec being the most complete in standard works. Montreal as far back as 1823, had several book stores, and a public library of 8,000 volumes, containing many valuable works, and, independent of this, there were two circulating libraries, the property of booksellers, both of which were tolerably well supplied with new books. [Footnote: Talbot's Canada, Vol. I., p. 77. But it appears that there was a circulating library at Quebec as far back as 1779, with 2,000 volumes; it was maintained till a few years ago, when its books were transferred to the Literary and Historical Society.] In this respect Montreal possessed for years decided advantages over York, for Mrs. Jameson tells us that when she arrived there ten years later, that town contained only one bookstore, in which drugs and other articles were also sold. Indeed, Mr. W. Lyon Mackenzie commenced life in Canada in the book and drug business with Mr. James Lesslie, the profits of the books going to the latter, and the profits of the drugs to the former. Subsequently, Mr. Mackenzie established a circulating library at Dundas, in connection with drugs, hardware, jewellery, and other miscellaneous wares, it being evidently impossible, in those days, to live by books alone. [Footnote: Lindsey's Life, pp. 36-7.] By 1836, however, even Mrs. Jameson, ready as she was to point out the defects of Canadian life, was obliged to acknowledge that Toronto had 'two good book-stores, with a fair circulating library.' Archdeacon Strachan and Chief Justice Robinson, according to the same author, had 'very pretty libraries.' Well-known gentlemen in the other Provinces had also well furnished libraries for those times.

We see in the articles contributed to the newspapers many evidences of careful writing and well digested reading. Literary and scientific societies now existed in all the large towns, though they necessarily depended for their support on a select few. Theatrical entertainments and concerts of a high order were not of unfrequent occurrence, for instance, we read in the Montreal papers of 1833 carefully-written notices of the performances of Mr. and Miss Kemble. The press also published lengthy criticisms of new publications, much more discriminating in some cases than the careless reviews of these later times, which seem too often written simply with the object of puffing a work, and not with a desire to cultivate a correct taste. We notice, too, that half a century ago there were gentlemen who thought they had an innate genius for writing manuals of arithmetic, and so forth, for the bewilderment of the Canadian youth. The literary tastes of the people were, then as now, fostered by the Boston and New York publishers; for example, we see lengthy notices of 'Harper's Family Library,' a series of cheap publications of standard works on History, Biography, Travels, &c., an invaluable acquisition to Canadians, the majority of whom could ill afford to pay the large prices then asked for English books. Several magazines began to be published in the East and West.

The first experiment of this kind was the *Canadian Magazine*, printed by N. Mower, in 1823, and subsequently published by Joseph Nickless, bookseller, opposite the Court House, Montreal. It was intended, in the words of the preface, 'as an archive for giving permanency to literary and scientific pursuits in the only British continental colony in the western hemisphere which has yet made any progress in settlement and cultivation.' The introduction is a very characteristic bit of writing, commencing as it does with a reference to the condition of 'man as a savage in mind and body,' and to the advance of the countries of ancient civilization in art and letters, until at last the reader is brought to appreciate the high object which the conductors had in view in establishing this new magazine—'to keep alive the heroic and energetic sentiment of our ancestors, their private virtues and public patriotism, and to form, for the example of posterity, a moral, an industrious, and loyal population.' The early following issues contained many well-written articles on Canadian subjects which give us some insight into the habits and tastes of the people, and are worthy of perusal by all those who take an interest in the old times of the colony. One particularly valuable feature was the digest of provincial news at the end of each number,—civil appointments, deaths, births and marriages, and army intelligence being deemed worthy of insertion. Among other things illustrative of social progress in 1823, we find notices of the first amateur concert given at Montreal in aid of a charitable object; of the establishment of the Quebec Historical Society, an event in the literary annals of Canada; of the foundation of the first circulating library in the City of Halifax, said to contain a number of valuable works. In 1824, H. A. Cunningham published, in Montreal, a rival publication, the *Canadian Review, and Literary and Historical Journal,* which appears to have excited the ire of the editor of the *Canadian Magazine,* for he devotes several pages of one issue to a criticism of its demerits. But these publications had only an ephemeral existence, and were succeeded by others. One of those was the *Museum,* edited by ladies in Montreal, in 1833. It contained some articles of merit, with a good deal of sentimental gush, [Footnote: The veteran editor of the *Quebec Mercury* thus pleasantly hit off this class of literature, always appreciated by boarding-school misses and milliners' apprentices: — '"The Cousins," written by M. — —, we candidly admit we did not encounter. When a man has arrived at that time of life when he is compelled to use spec— —no, not so bad as that, but *lunettes,* in order to accommodate the text to his eyes, and finds at the conclusion of an article such a passage as the following: "Beneath that knoll, at the foot of that weeping ash, side by side, in the bosom of one grave lie Reginald and Charlotte de Conrci"—when a semi-centenarian meets such a passage in such a situation, it is a loss of time for him to turn back and threading way through the mazes of the story.'] such as one found in the keepsakes and other gift books of those days. The first magazine of ability in the West appears to have been the *Canadian Magazine,* edited by Mr. Sibbald, and published at Toronto in 1833. The next periodical, which lasted many years, was the *Literary Garland,* published in Montreal, in conjunction with Mr. John Gibson, [Footnote: These two gentlemen were long associated in the partnership, widely known throughout Canada, as that of Lovell & Gibson, parliamentary printers.] by that veteran publisher, John Lovell, a gentleman to whom the country owes much for his zeal and enterprise in all such literary matters. All these facts were illustrative of the growth of literary and cultured taste throughout the Provinces, even in those early times. But it must be admitted that then, as now, the intellectual progress of Canada was very slow compared with that of the United States, where, during the times of which I am writing, literature was at last promising to be a profession, Cooper, Irving and

Poe having already won no little celebrity at home and abroad. It was not till the Canadas were re-united and population and wealth poured into the country that culture began to be more general. Sixteen years after Mrs. Jameson published her account of Canada, another writer [Footnote: W. H. Kigston. 1852. 2 vols] visited Toronto, and wrote in very flattering terms of the appearance of the city, and the many evidences of taste he noticed in the streets and homes of its people. At that time he tells us there were 'five or six large booksellers' shops, equal to any in the larger towns of England, and some of whom were publishers also.' Mr. Maclear had at that time 'published two very well-got-up volumes on Canada, by Mr. W. H. Smith, and was also the publisher of the *Anglo-American Magazine*, a very creditably conducted periodical.' Now, in this same City of Toronto, there are some forty stationers' and booksellers' establishments, small and large; whilst there are about one hundred altogether in the leading cities of the Provinces. Of the libraries, I shall have occasion to write some pages further on.

Since 1840, Canadians have made many ambitious efforts in the walks of literature, though only a few works have achieved a reputation beyond our own country. Nova Scotia can claim the credit of giving birth to two men whose works, though in very different fields of intellectual effort, have won for them no little distinction abroad. 'Sam Slick' may now be considered an English classic, new editions of which are still published from year to year and placed on the bookseller's shelves with the works of Fielding, Smollett, Butler and Barham. The sayings and doings of the knowing clockmaker were first published by Mr. Howe in the columns of the old *Nova Scotia*, still published as the weekly edition of the Halifax *Chronicle*, for the purpose of preserving some good stories and anecdotes of early colonial life. Like many good things that appear in the Canadian press, the judge's humorous effort would, no doubt, have been forgotten long before these times, had not the eminent publisher, Mr. Richard Bentley, seen the articles and printed them in book form. The humour of the work soon established the reputation of the author, and together with his companionable qualities made the 'old judge' a favourite when he left his native province and settled in England, where he lived and died, like Cowley, Thomson, Pope, and other men known to fame, on the banks of the Thames. The comments of 'Sam Slick' are full of keen humour, and have a moral as well. When first published, the work was not calculated to make him popular with certain classes of his countrymen, impatient of the satire which touched off weaknesses and follies in the little social and political world of those laggard times; but now that the habits of the people have changed, and the Nova Scotia of the Clockmaker exists no longer, except perhaps in some lonely corner; every one laughs at his humorous descriptions of the slow old times, and confesses, that if things were as Sam has portrayed them in his quaint way, he only acted the part of a true moralist in laying them bare to the world, and aiming at them the pointed shafts of his ready satire. The work is likely to have a more enduring reputation than the mere mechanical humour of the productions of 'Mark Twain.' Many of his sayings, like 'soft sawder,' have entered into our every day conversation.

The other distinguished Nova Scotian is the learned Principal of McGill College. Professor Dawson is a native of the County of Pictou, which has given birth to many men of ability in divinity, letters and politics. At an early age the natural bent of his talent carried him into the rich, unbroken field that the geology of his native province offered in those days to scientists. The two visits he paid with Sir Charles Lyell through Nova Scotia, gave him admirable opportunities of comparing notes with that distinguished geologist, and no doubt did much to encourage him in the pursuit of an attractive, though hardly remunerative, branch of study. The result was his first work, 'Acadian Geology,' which was at once accepted by *savants* everywhere as a valuable contribution to geological literature. His subsequent works—'The Story of the Earth and Man,' 'Fossil Man,' 'The Origin of the World,' and his numerous contributions to scientific periodicals, have aided to establish his reputation as a sound scholar and tasteful writer, as easily understood by the ordinary reader as by the student of geological lore. Moreover, his religious instincts have kept him free from that scepticism and infidelity into which scientists like himself are so apt to fall, as the result of their close studies of natural science; and his later works have all been written with the object of reconciling the conclusions of Science with the teachings of Scripture—a very difficult task discharged in a spirit of candour, liberality and fairness, which has won the praise of his most able adversaries.

A great deal of poetry has been written in Canadian periodicals, and now and then certainly we come across productions displaying much poetic taste as well as rhythmic skill. The only work of a high order that has attracted some attention abroad, is 'Saul,' a Drama, by Charles Heavysege, who died in Montreal not long since, a humble worker on the daily press. The leading English reviews, at the time of its appearance, acknowledged that 'it is undoubtedly one of the most remarkable works ever written out of Great Britain;' and yet, despite the grandeur of the subject, and the poetical and dramatic power, as well as the psychological analysis displayed in its conception and execution, this production of a local reporter, gifted with undoubted genius, is only known to a few Canadians. 'Saul,' like Milton's great epic, now-a-days, is only admired by a few, and never read by the many. Charles Sangster has also given us a very pleasing collection of poems, in which, like Wordsworth, he illustrates his love for nature by graceful, poetic descriptions of the St. Lawrence and the Saguenay. That a pure poetic vein runs through the minds of not a few of our writers, can be seen by a perusal of the poems contributed for some years to the CANADIAN MONTHLY, *Scribner's*, and other publications, by L'Esperance, Watson, Griffin, Carroll Ryan, 'Fidelis,' John Reade, Charles Roberts, Mrs. Seymour McLean, and C. P. Mulvany; the volume recently published by the latter writer is undoubtedly a good illustration of the poetic talent that exists among the cultured classes of our people.

As to Canadian novels and romances, there is very little to say; for though there have been many attempts at fiction, the performance has, on the whole, been weak in the extreme. In historic romance, only three works of merit have been so far produced; and these are 'Wacousta,' written by Major Richardson, in 1833; 'Le Bastonnais,' by M. L'Esperance, and 'Le Chien d'Or,' by Mr. Kirby, since 1867—during the long interval of nearly forty years between these works, not a single romance worth reading was published in Canada. These three books, however, are written with spirit, and recall the masterpieces of fiction. In novels, illustrative of ordinary life in the Colonies, we know of no works that anybody remembers except those by Miss Louisa Murray, the author of 'The Cited Curate,' and 'The Settlers of Long Arrow,' who, at all events, writes naturally, and succeeds in investing her story with a vein of interest. The late Professor De Mille gave us two well-written productions in 'Helena's Household,' a 'Tale of Rome in the First Century,' and 'The Dodge Club Abroad;' but his later works did not keep up the promise of his earlier efforts, for they never rose beyond slavish imitations of the ingenious plots of Wilkie Collins and his school. Yet they were above the ordinary Canadian novel, and had many readers in the United States and Canada.

In History, much has been attempted. Every one who can write an article in a country newspaper thinks he is competent to give the world a history of our young Dominion in some shape or other; and yet, when we come to review the results, it can hardly be said that the literary success is remarkable. The history of Canada, as a whole, has yet to be written, and it most be admitted that the task has its difficulties. The first era has its picturesque features, which may attract an eloquent writer, but the field has in a large measure been already occupied with great fidelity and ability by that accomplished historian, Francis Parkman, of Boston. The subsequent history, under the English *regime*, labours under the disadvantage of want of unity, and being for the most part a record of comparatively insignificant political controversy. To the outside world such a history has probably no very great attraction, and consequently could bring an author no great measure of reputation. Yet, if a Canadian imbued with true patriotism, content with the applause of his own countrymen, should devote to the task much patient research, and a graceful style, and while leaving out all petty and unimportant details, should bring into bold relief the salient and noteworthy features of the social and political development of Canada, such a writer would lift Canadian history out of that slough of dullness into which so many have succeeded in throwing it in their efforts to immortalise themselves rather than their country. Nor can it be truly said that to trace the successive stages in a nation's growth, is a task uninteresting or unimportant, even to the great world beyond us. But Canada has as yet no national importance; she is only in the colonial transition, stage, and her influence on other peoples is hardly yet appreciable So it happens, that whilst the history of a small state in Europe like Holland, Belgium, or Denmark, may win a writer a world-wide reputation, as was the case with Motley, on the other hand, the history of a colonial community is only associated in the minds of the foreign public with petty political conflicts, and not with those great movements of humanity which have affected so deeply the political and social fabric of European States.

All that, however, by way of parenthesis. Garneau's history, of which we have a fair translation, remains the best work of the kind, but it is not a history of Canada—simply of one section and of one class of the population. Hannay's 'History of Acadia' is also a work which displays research, and skill in arranging the materials, as well as a pleasing, readable style. Such works as Murdoch's 'History of Nova Scotia,' Dr. Canniff's Bay of Quinte, Dr. Scadding's 'Toronto of Old' are very valuable in the way of collecting facts and data from dusty archives and from old pioneers, thus saving the future historian much labour. The last mentioned book is one of the most interesting works of the class ever published in this country, and shows what an earnest, enthusiastic antiquarian can do for the English-speaking races in Canada, in perpetuating the memories and associations that cling to old landmarks. Like Dr. Scadding in Toronto, Mr. James Lemoine has delved industriously among the historic monuments of Quebec, and made himself the historian *par excellence* of that interesting old city. To him the natural beauty of the St. Lawrence and its historic and legendary lore are as familiar as were the picturesque scenery and the history of Scotland to Sir Walter Scott. Both Mr. Lemoine and Dr. Scadding illustrate what may be done in other cities and towns of Canada by an enthusiastic student of their annals, who would not aim too high, but be content with the reputation of local historians or antiquarians. We cannot lose any time in committing to paper the recollections of those old settlers who are fast dying out among us. 'The Scot in British North America,' by Mr. W. J. Rattray, is an attempt—and a most meritorious one—to illustrate the history of the progress of a class who have done so much for the prosperity of this country. Historical bodies, like the New England Historical Society, can do a great deal to preserve the records of old times. The Quebec Literary Historical Society, founded as long ago as 1824, under the auspices of the Governor-General of the time, Lord Dalhousie, has done a good work with the small means at its command in this direction, and it is satisfactory to know that a similar institution has at last been established in Halifax, where there ought to be much interesting material in the possession of old families, whose founders came from New England or the "old country" in the troublous times of the American Revolution.

Reviewing generally works of a miscellaneous class, we find several that have deservedly won for the authors a certain position in Canadian literature. For instance, Colonel Denison's works on Cavalry, one of which gained a prize offered by the Emperor of Russia, illustrate certainly the fertility and acuteness of the Canadian intellect when it is stimulated to some meritorious performance in a particular field. Mrs. Moodie's 'Roughing it in the Bush' is an evidence of the interest that may be thrown around the story of the trials and struggles of settlers in the wilderness, when the writer describes the life naturally and effectively. [Footnote: In the course of my readings of old files in the Parliamentary library, I came across this reference to the early literary efforts of this lady, whose pen in later times has contributed so much charming poetry and prose to Canadian publications, serial and general: 'The editor of the New York *Albion* has had the good fortune to obtain as contributor to his poetical columns the name of Susanna Moodie, better known among the admirers of elegiac poetry, in her days of celibate life, as Susanna Strickland. From the specimen with which she has furnished Dr. Bartlett of her poetic ardour, we are happy to find that neither the Canadian atmosphere nor the circumstances attendant upon the alteration of her name, have dimmed the light of that Muse which, in past years, engaged many of our juvenile hours with pleasure and profit.'—Montreal *Gazette*, 1833.] Mr. Charles Lindsey has given us, among other works, a life of Wm. Lyon Mackenzie,—with whom he was connected by marriage—valuable for its historical accuracy and moderate spirit. Mr. George Stewart has in 'Evenings in the Library' illustrated how earnestly and conscientiously he has studied English and American literature. Dr. Daniel Wilson, since he has made Canada his home, has continued to illustrate the versatility of his knowledge and the activity of his intellect by his works on 'Prehistoric Man,' and 'Recollections of Edinburgh,' besides his many contributions to the proceedings of learned societies and the pages of periodicals, Mr. Fennings Taylor, an accomplished official of Parliament, has given us a number of gracefully-written essays on Episcopalian dignitaries and Canadian statesmen, though he has had to labour in most cases with the difficulty of reviewing the career of men still in life, whose political merit is still a point in the opinion of parties. Mr. Alpheus Todd, the well-known librarian of Parliament, has been without a rival in the dependencies of Great Britain, in his particular line of constitutional studies. For over a quarter of a century he has been accumulating precedent upon precedent, until his mind is a remarkable store-house of well-digested data, from which he has illustrated the growth of Parliamentary institutions in Great Britain and her Colonies. His style is remarkably clear and logical, — though the character of his works and the plan adopted in their execution, are unfavourable to literary finish, — and even those who may not agree with his conclusions, on certain constitutional points, will give full credit to the conscientiousness of his researches and the sincerity of his purpose. His 'Parliamentary Government in England' was described in the *Edinburgh Review* as 'one of the most useful and complete works which has yet appeared on the practical operation of the British Constitution.' It says much for our system of Government, that it has been able to stimulate the intellectual faculties of a Canadian writer to the production of such thoughtful, erudite works. They are a natural outcome of the interest which all classes of our people take in questions of a political bearing. They illustrate the mental activity which, from the earliest times in our history, has been devoted to the study of political and constitutional questions, and which has hitherto for the most part found expression only in the press or in the legislatures of the different provinces. Works of constitutional authority like those of Hallam, May, Stubbs, and Todd must emanate naturally from the student, removed from the turmoil and excitement of political contests, rather than from the politician and statesman, whose mind can hardly ever find that freedom from bias which would give general confidence in his works, if indeed he could ever find time to produce them.

And here we may appropriately refer to the contributions made to Colonial literature by the eminent men who have assisted in giving Canada her present political and industrial status. The great speeches of Canadian statesmen must nearly all be sought in the old files of newspapers deposited in our libraries; but as a rule the chief interest that now attaches to these speeches is the light they throw on the history of the past. The opportunities which Canadian statesmen have had of making great oratorical efforts have not been frequent in dependencies where the questions have necessarily been for the most part of purely local importance and of a very practical character. Yet when subjects of large constitutional or national importance have come up for discussion, the debates prove that Canadian intellects display a comprehensiveness of knowledge and a power of argument worthy of a larger arena. Some of Sir Alexander Galt's speeches, in bringing down the Budget in old times, were characterized by that masterly arrangement of statistics which has made Mr. Gladstone so famous in the House of Commons. Sir John Macdonald's speech explaining the Washington Treaty, in 1872, was remarkable for its logical arrangement and its illustrations of the analytical power and the varied knowledge of that eminent statesman, who, in the intervals of leisure, has always been a student of general literature. Mr. Blake's speeches afford abundant evidence of the brilliant talent of a public man who is both a student of books as well as of politics, and who, were the tendency of Parliamentary oratory something higher than mere practical debate, could rise fully to the height of some great argument. But oratory, in the real sense of the art, cannot exist in our system of government in a Colonial dependency where practical results are immediately sought for. It consequently follows that the speeches which interest us to-day lose their attraction when the object has been gained. Both Mr. Howe and Mr. McGee were able to invest their great addresses with a charm which still clings to them when we take them up. The reason is, they were, like Gladstone and Disraeli, both *litterateurs* who studied their subjects in the library, among the great masters of eloquence and statesmanship, and were thus able to throw around a great question the flowers of a highly cultivated mind. But even Mr. Howe's most memorable speeches of old times would perhaps be hardly appreciated in the cold practical arena in which our public business is now transacted. Yet it cannot be said that the Legislature is no field to display the highest qualities of intellectual activity because it is no longer possible to indulge in those nights of poetic fancy or those brilliant perorations which are now confined to the pulpit or lecture-hall. The intellectual strength of the country must be of no mean order when it can give us statesmen like Sir Charles Tupper and Mr. Mackenzie, whose best speeches are admirable illustrations of logical arrangement and argumentative power. And, it may be added, with respect to the present House, that no previous Parliament, entrusted with the control of the affairs of Canada, has comprised a larger number of gentlemen, distinguished not only for their practical comprehension of the wants of this country, but for their wide attainments and general culture.

When we come to sum up the literary results of the century that has passed since the two races entered conjointly on the material and intellectual development of Canada, it will be seen that there has been a steady movement forward. It must be admitted that Canada has not yet produced any works which show a marked originality of thought. Some humorous writings, a few good poems, one or two histories, some scientific and constitutional productions, are alone known to a small reading public outside of Canada. Striking originality can hardly be developed to any great extent in a dependency which naturally, and perhaps wisely in some cases, looks for all its traditions and habits of thought to a parent state. It is only with an older condition of society, when men have learned at last to think as well as to act for themselves, to originate rather than to reproduce, that there can be a national literature. The political development of Canada within forty years affords forcible evidence of the expansion of the political ideas of our public men, who are no longer tormented by the dread of what others say of them, but legislate solely with respect to the internal necessities of the country; and the same development is now going on in other departments of intellectual life, and affords additional evidence of our national growth. It must also be remembered that there is a mental activity among the intelligent classes of the country, in itself as significant as the production of great works. Like our American neighbours, the mass of Canadians is able to think intelligently, and come generally to a right conclusion, on all matters of local concern; in this respect, no comparison need be made with the mass of Englishmen or Frenchmen in the Old World, for the social and educational facilities within the reach of the people of this country, give them undoubted advantages over others. It is only necessary to consider the number of pamphlets and volumes on matters affecting Canada, that annually issue from the press in this country, to show the existence of a mental activity in entire harmony with the industrial progress of the country. [Footnote: For instance, we find in Morgan's 'Annual Register' for 1879, that during that year there were no less than 166 publications issued from the press, of which 17 were poetic; 12 historical; 15 educational; 17 legal; 24 religious; 66 miscellaneous, &c. Some of these were of considerable merit, as 'Tasse's Pioneers,' F. Taylor's 'Are Legislatures Parliaments?' Frechette's Poems, Hannay's 'Acadia,' &c. In this connection it may be interesting to add that the Parliamentary Library contains some 1,400 copies of pamphlets, bound in 200 volumes, since Confederation, and that the total number of original Canadian publications registered since that time is over 1,500 — only a few of the pamphlets being registered copyright. The Parliamentary Library, however, is very defective yet in Canadian books, papers and pamphlets. Laval University has a far more valuable collection. We ought to have a National Library like the British Museum, where all Canadian publications can have a place. Strange as it may seem, only a few copies of old Canadian papers can be found in the Ottawa Library. Yet, if a little money were spent and trouble. taken, a valuable collection could be procured from private individuals throughout the Dominion.] It is fair then to argue that the intellectual progress of a country like Canada must not be measured solely by the production of great works which have been stamped with the approval of the outside literary world, on whose verdict, it must of course be admitted, depends true fame. We must also look to the signs of general culture that are now exhibited on all sides, compared with a quarter of a century ago, when the development of material interests necessarily engrossed all the best faculties of the people. The development of higher education, together with the formation of Art Schools, Museums, and Literary Societies, is illustrative of the greater mental activity of all classes. The paintings of O'Brien and Verner are pleasing evidences of the growth of art in a country where, hitherto, but few pictures of merit have even been imported. It is no longer considered a sign of good taste to cover the walls with oils and chromes whose chief value is the tawdry, showy gilt which encases them and makes so loud a display on the walls of the *nouveaux riches*. In the style of public buildings and private dwellings, there is a remarkable improvement within twenty years, to indicate not only the increase of national and individual wealth, but the growth of a cultured taste. The interior decorations, too, show a desire to imitate the modern ideas that prevail abroad; and in this respect every year must witness a steady advance, according as our people travel more in the older countries in Europe and study the fashions of the artistic and intellectual world. There are even now in prosaic, practical Canada, some men and women who fully appreciate the aesthetic ideal that the poet Morris would achieve in the form, harmony, and decoration of domestic furniture. If such aesthetic ideas could only be realized in the decoration of our great public edifices, the Parliamentary buildings at Ottawa, for instance, the national taste would certainly be improved. At present huge portraits of politicians, who by intrinsic merit or political favour have become speakers, stare down from the walls in solitary grandeur, and already begin to overcrowd each other. We search in vain for allegorical paintings by eminent Canadian artists, or monuments of illustrious statesmen, such as we see in the Capitol at Washington, or in the elegant structure nearly completed at Albany.

In one respect we are still much behind hand, and that is in our Public Libraries. The library of the Parliament of Canada still remains the only institution worthy of much notice in the Dominion. It was certainly an event in the history of literary culture in Canada when this library was moved into the edifice whose architectural beauty is in itself an illustration of the rapid advance in taste of the Dominion. As one looks up at its chaste, vaulted ceiling, which lights the tiers of volumes, arranged in a circle, one recalls the now forgotten poem of Crabbe, that ardent lover of books:—

> Come, Child of Care! to make thy soul serene,
> Approach the treasures of this tranquil scene;
> Survey the dome, and, as the doors unfold,
> The soul's best cure, in all her cares, behold!
> Where mental wealth the poor in thought may find,
> And mental physic the diseased in mind.

* * * * *

> With awe, around these silent walks we tread;
> These are the lasting mansions of the dead:—

"The dead!" Methinks a thousand tongues reply:
"These are the tombs of such as cannot die!
"Crowned with eternal fame, they sit sublime
"And laugh at all the little strife of time."

But whilst we pay this tribute to its architectural grace, one won-
ders at the same time at the shortsightedness which has sacrificed
everything to appearance, and given us a building not even equal to
existing demands—as if a library was a thing of the present, not to
increase with the intellectual requirements of the country. As it is
now, the library contains only some 100,000 volumes, many of
which have no particular value. The American and Canadian de-
partment is confessedly inferior in many respects, although we
ought to excel in that particular. Of late years, the annual grant has
been extremely small, and chiefly devoted to the purchase of books
for the law branch, for the especial benefit of lawyers engaged in the
Supreme Court. But we have as yet no Free Libraries like those in
the United States, of which the Boston Library is a notable illustration. [Footnote: Boston, twenty years ago, spent and spent well, in
founding her great free library, more than two dollars for each man,
woman, and child within her limits, and she has sustained it to this
day with great spirit and liberality. That library has now more than
360,000 volumes, and her citizens in 1879 took to their homes more
than 1,160,000 volumes. Many smaller places in New England and
elsewhere, not without careful investigation, have followed her
example, finding in the practical results of her 20 years' work, proof
satisfactory to their tax-payers, that a free library is a profitable
investment of public money, while in the West the great cities of
Cincinnati, Chicago, and St. Louis, with Western free-handed energy, have already free libraries on such a scale that one at least of
them bids fair to rank among the greatest in the world—*Scribner's
Monthly* for September, 1880, where the advantages of a free library
are very tersely shown.] But, nevertheless, the reading facilities of
the people generally have increased very largely within two decades. At the present time, as far as we can estimate from the information within reach, there are some 130,000 volumes in the Parliamentary Libraries of the Dominion, 700,000 in the Universities, Col-

leges and Schools—all of which are necessarily of a limited professional class—and 140,000 in Mechanics' Institutes and Literary Societies. The grand total of library and prize books despatched to the Public Schools of the Province of Ontario alone within twenty-five years is over one million and a quarter of volumes—comprising of course books of an educational character, but nevertheless valuable in laying the foundation of general culture, and bringing the means of acquiring knowledge to sections where otherwise such facilities would be wanting. Last year, the value of the books imported into Canada amounted to about a million of dollars, or an increase of about 30 per cent. in ten years. Literary and Scientific Institutes are increasing in number, and some are doing a useful, if not a national work: the Quebec Historical Society, referred to on a previous page, the Toronto Canadian Institute, which has made not a few useful contributions to science and literature, and the Institut Canadien which has erected in Ottawa one of the handsomest structures yet raised in Canada by a literary association. In Ontario there are also some 100 Mechanics Institutes, including nearly 11,000 members, with an aggregate of 118,000 volumes in the libraries; [Footnote: 'Address of Mr. James Young, President of Mechanics' Institutes Association of Ontario (*Globe*, Sept. 24th, 1880).] and it is satisfactory to learn that institutions which may have an important influence on the industrial classes are to be placed on a more efficient basis. These facts illustrate that we are making progress in the right direction; but what we want, above all things, are public libraries, to which all classes may have free access, in the principal centres of population. The rich men of this country can devote a part of their surplus wealth to no more patriotic purpose than the establishment of such libraries in the places where they live, and in that way erect a monument for themselves far more honourable than any that may be achieved by expenditures on purely selfish objects. All through the New England and Central States we meet with such illustrations of private generosity, but there are few similar examples in Canada. Perhaps the handsome contribution recently made by Mr. Redpath towards the establishment of a museum in connection with McGill College—itself a memorial of private generosity—is a favourable augury of what we may often look for in the future, as the number of our wealthy men increase and they become more alive to the intellectual wants of those around them.

In the columns of our ablest journals there is a growing tendency to devote more space to the discussion of literary, artistic and scientific topics which are engaging attention in the world of thought The publication of a periodical like the *Bystander* may justly be considered an event in the political and literary annals of this country. It illustrates the desire that exists for independent political criticism amid the intense conflict of party opinion; and even those who cannot agree with the views of the eminent gentleman who conducts this work will frankly admit the originality and independence of thought in all he says. But it is not only as a political writer that Mr. Smith is doing good service to this country; every one who reads his reviews of current events cannot fail to profit by the study of his graceful style as well as by the versatility of his knowledge on all the social, political and economic questions that are engaging attention at home or abroad. The pages of the *Canadian Monthly* have also for some time shown that there is coming to the front a number of writers of considerable intellectual power on the leading social and religious problems to which so many able thinkers are devoting themselves now-a-days. Herbert Spencer has his disciples and defenders, who prove themselves no contemptible adversaries of the orthodox school of religion. Very few of us probably sympathize with these modern iconoclasts who would destroy all motive for right doing in this world, by breaking down human faith in the existence of one Supreme Being; but, at the same time, no one can deny the earnestness and ability these writers bring to their work. It is quite obvious that such able thinkers as Mr. Spencer and his followers in Canada, with Mr. Le Sueur at their head, cannot be 'snubbed' cavalierly by the professed teachers of religion. The tendency of modern thought, a wave of which has reached us, is undoubtedly in the direction of bringing all subjects, however sacred, to the crucial test of argument, fact and experience, and our religious guides must not think they will prevail by the exhibit of mere contemptuous indifference to the free thought that prevails around them. If our great theological schools and seats of learning are to prove themselves equal to the demands of the present day, it will be by moving out of their grooves of worn-out tradition and routine, and by enlarging their teachings so that the men they send out into the world may be more equal than most of them appear now to meet in argument the Positivist, Rationalist and Materialist, or whatever the disciple of the modern schools of philosophy may call himself. The man of true liberality and faith in the truth of his religious principles must be fully prepared to allow the freest expression of opinion, however antagonistic it may appear to the true happiness of society. This very conflict of ideas and arguments between such opposite schools of opinion must, in the end, evolve the truth, and necessarily give additional stimulus to intellectual thought in this country, where, so far, there has been a great dearth of original thinkers to elevate us above purely selfish, material interests.

In the natural order of things, the next half century ought to witness a far larger development of the intellect of this country. We have already seen that, with the progress of the Dominion in population and wealth, education has been stimulated to a remarkable degree, journalism has become more of a profession, and not only have several books, of more than ordinary value and merit, been produced in various departments of knowledge, but there are already signs of a spirit of intellectual emulation which must, sooner or later, have its full fruition. If Canada makes the material progress within the next few decades that her people hope, and her statesmen are endeavouring to accomplish, in the face, no doubt, of many difficulties, we may confidently look forward to a corresponding intellectual development. So much practical work of immediate importance has to be performed in a comparatively new country like this, that native talent has naturally found chief expression in politics, the professions, and the press; but with greater wealth, and an older condition of society, literature, science, and art, will be cultivated to a far larger extent. 'It was amid the ruins of the Capitol,' says Gibbon, 'that I first conceived the idea of writing the "History of the Roman Empire."' Such a work could not have been written among the forests of Canada, while men were labouring with the many difficulties of a pioneer existence. But with the greater opportunities of leisure and culture necessarily opening up to us in the future, Canadians may yet have a literature, not merely imitative, as at present, but creative and original. It is stated somewhere in an old English review of American literature, that on this new continent we can hardly expect the rich fruition which springs from that deep, humanized soil of the old world, which has for ages been enriched by the ripe droppings of a fertile national life, where, in the words of an American poet, —

One half the soil has walked the rest,
In poets, heroes, martyrs, sages.

It is certainly true that the beauty and grandeur of external nature alone will never inspire the highest and deepest writings; but human life with its manifold experiences, its glooms and glories, sorrows and rejoicings, pains, pleasures and aspirations. Every rood of ground in the old communities of Europe has its historic associations to point many a moral and adorn many a tale. Yet if this America of ours has a history only of yesterday, it, too, has its memories and associations to stimulate the genius of history, poetry and romance. Already in the first century of American literature have poets and historians and artists appeared to rival those of the older civilization of the world. The works of Parkman and Longfellow illustrate that there is, even in the early history and traditions of Canada, much to evoke the interest of the great world beyond us, when a writer brings to the task the genius of a true poet or the brilliancy of an accomplished historian. If our soil is new, yet it may produce fruits which will bear a rich flavour of their own, and may please the palate of even those surfeited with the hothouse growth of older lands. Hawthorne, Emerson, Howells, Bret Harte, Sam Slick, are among many writers who illustrate the raciness and freshness of American production. Nor let it be forgotten that American and Canadian, in 'the fresh woods and pastures new' of this continent, have an equal heritage with the people of the British Islands in that rich, humanized soil which has borne such rare intellectual fruit. We, too, may enjoy its bounteous gifts and gather inspiration from its treasures of 'English undefiled,' although we live in another land whose history dawned but yesterday, and where the soil is almost virgin.

In this land there is a future full of promise for literature as for industry. Our soil speaks to the millions of poor in the old countries of the world of boundless hope. Here there is no ancient system of social exclusiveness to fix a limit to the intellectual progress of the proletariat. Political freedom rests on a firm, broad basis of general education. Our political constitution is not alienated from the intellect of the country, but its successful working depends entirely on the public intelligence. As our political horizon widens, and a more expansive national existence opens before us, so must our intellectual life become not only more vigorous, but more replete with evidences of graceful culture:

'For through all the ages one increasing purpose runs,
And the thoughts of men are widened with the process of the suns.'